Snow Falls

CORINA ZURCHER
&
MARYANN BECKMAN

Based on the Christmas Songs
Little Red Guitar and *Christmas Recipe* by Ray Fontenault
&
Tiny Angels by Ray Fontenault and Galen Breen

ISBN: 0991172426
ISBN-13: 978-09911724-2-9

NEVERMORE PUBLICATIONS, LLC ®

www.snowfalls.doraymusicpromotions.com

DEDICATION

To those who carry Christmas in their hearts all year long,
this is for you.

"Be not forgetful to entertain strangers: for thereby some have entertained angels unawares."
-Hebrews 13:2

1

It was coming. They sensed it. They felt it. They *knew*. In hearts and homes all across the world, they could hear the drumbeat of time announcing the changing of the season, marching across the foliage of autumn gold, rusty orange and muddy brown, drowning out the wind and rain of Fall while rousing the hibernating season of Winter. As they turned their ear to the sound of percussion, the cold wind breathed forth its first snow, and in reply, their hearts began to flutter in anticipation of what the harkened season would soon be bringing as the days grew short and the nights grew long.

For the young at heart, it was the time of season when *he* would come—the jolly old man with the long white beard adorned in a suit of scarlet velour, bearing prized gifts from hopeful letters—*Santa Claus*. For the old in spirit, it was the reminder of a different *He* that had come long ago bringing the weary soul an even greater gift of timeless peace in a land of despair. His name...*Emmanuel*.

Christmas is a time of cheerful songs and letters, piles of presents and candy-filled stockings, pine-scented trees and wreathes, and warm, cozy fires. It is a cherished time to visit with family and friends over a hot cup of cocoa; a welcome excuse to resurrect timeless traditions of baking and holiday meals, attending boutiques and bazaars, and embarking on road trips down adorned streets that

1

rivaled any Christmas Town the North Pole had ever seen—memories that filled the days until December 25th finally arrived.

But although the holiday season was beautiful to behold, it was by no means perfect. There were those caught up in the commercial aspect of Christmas, where forced gift-giving stripped the desire to celebrate its true meaning in the end. And while it is a season of joy for some, it could be an ocean of loneliness for others—a reminder of heartache and pain magnified by a season filled with family and love.

And as the earthly angel stood on an isolated street in the middle of a town called Snow Falls, he could hear the howling of lonely souls yearning for peace just as strongly as he could see the burning, joyous hearts of men glowing in excitement, lighting up the households all along the row.

He had heard such dueling thunder in the heavens before—they all had—as if the multitude of praise and honor of the faithful challenged the cries and yearnings of the hopeless to show that no matter what side of the field you were on, some day either one would be heard. And heard they were indeed—*all* of them—for his Father had heard His people's cry, and answered it by sending the world His greatest gift—His love.

"And lo, the angel of the Lord came upon them, and the glory of the Lord shone around them; and they were 'sore afraid. And the angel said to them, 'Fear not: for behold, I bring unto you good tidings of great joy, which shall be to all people. For unto you is born this day in the City of David a Savior, which is Christ the Lord."

It was an answer indeed.

Walking along the streets, seeing the homes adorned with Christmas lights and festive decorations of Frosty, candy canes, Santa and Rudolph, the angel smiled in amusement thinking back to that first Christmas. There were no twinkling lights or Christmas trees then, no elves or snowmen. There was a stable filled with hay, swaddling clothes, and a manger. There were no carolers gathered on front porches asking for figgy pudding, but stable animals that neighed and stomped all around the one true king.

The angel approached a small church, watching as various patrons set up a life-sized Nativity—his favorite decoration. He watched as the statues were perfectly situated all around the manger, surrounding the tiny babe. His eyes absorbed the bright colors painted on the robes of the figurines, taking in the craftsmanship of each and every statue until he sees the angel. His eyes twinkled as he peered at the ivory robes and large white wings, focusing on the stoic expression painted on the angel's face. He smiled to himself knowing that none of them were stoic that first Christmas. No, they were exuberant, shouting from the heavens as the shepherds down below looked at them in awe as they heralded the birth of the Almighty's son. He, himself, had fallen to his knees.

One of the church patrons, an elderly gentleman, catches the earthly angel gazing at the crèche. "Good evening to you!"

"Good evening to you, sir."

"I see you like our statue. Beautiful angel, isn't it?"

"Yes, he is."

"I always wondered what it would be like to see one."

"An angel?" He laughs. "You mean, you never have?"

The elderly man looks back at him. "Not that I'm aware of."

"How do you know?"

The man's eyes narrow at the question. "One would know if they'd seen the likes of this." He points his finger at the statue. "I've heard most people fall down in terror the moment they see an angel."

The earthly angel grins. "Why is that, you suppose?"

The man looks at him in shock, "Because they're giants! Filled with blazing fire! They could blind you, you know, walking around in all that light!"

"Geez, all that. And you still want to see one?"

The old man ponders his question, "Come to think of it, I changed my mind. My hair would get whiter than it already is. And my wife thinks it's white enough already."

"I'd call it silver."

The man chuckles and turns back to the statue. "Nah, this here statue is good enough for me if that's all I'm ever going to get to see in this lifetime."

The earthly angel's eyes twinkled even brighter as he looked at the elderly man staring at the molded being. He could see the wheels in the man's head spinning as he seemed to still be imagining what it would be like to actually see a real one.

"You know what I think?"

"Hmm?"

"I think you'll see your angel one day, but he won't blind you. He'll help you see. Have a good evening."

The earthly angel nods to the angel statue in mock salute and walks on, leaving the elderly man in befuddled silence before turning back to constructing the Nativity scene.

The angel rounds a corner that leads directly onto Main Street. The entire row is decorated in lights of every color as wreathes and garland hang from the lampposts. Parents and children hustle and bustle in and out of the small shops carrying bags of gifts in their arms. A man dressed as Santa Claus rings the Salvation Army bell on the corner directly across from him. The angel stops and observes all the passersby as they walk swiftly past the Santa without a turn of their head. He narrows his eyes at the red pail with a look of determination. The angel lifts his head and makes eye contact with a man walking down the street moving directly toward the Santa.

The man locks eyes with the angel and suddenly tosses a few coins in the red pail as he walks by. More men and women suddenly walk past the Santa, dropping their spare change into the collection box, eyeing the earthly angel, trying to understand the sudden need to reach into their pockets at that exact moment in time to drop it into the red pail. All they seemed to understand was that the handsome young man smiling at them as they did so, seemed to fill them with a sense of peace as they walked by. They could not help but smile back as his benevolent presence seemed to evoke spontaneous goodwill in all who were lucky enough to cross his path. And the more people that passed him, the more contagious the giving became. More people continued to toss money into the red pail, causing the Santa Claus to ring his bell louder and longer as he thanked the passersby. The Santa sees the handsome, young angel grinning from ear to ear.

"Merry Christmas!"

"Merry Christmas to you!"

More citizens drop their loose change in the bright red pail. Satisfied, the angel walks down the street toward a small bridge that overlooks the local ice pond. He remembered this pond. He had been here before, long ago, on a different mission in a different time.

Snow Falls.

It was not a remarkable town in any way. It was not known for any particular industry. It was a town wedged between the city and the country. A town where life was a little bit slower, a little bit quieter and overall, a little bit kinder.

The angel looks out across the ice pond to a large building standing on a small hill, reaching three stories high. He crosses the bridge and moves toward the entrance, observing the barren trees with dissatisfaction. He nods at the challenge, as if the desolate trees were metaphor for the souls that rested inside. He was sent to the earth off a single prayer from a man who lived in that building. It was a cry for forgiveness, a plea for peace and mercy, a request that had yet to be answered.

A request indeed.

Looking up at the second story window, he could see the man's shadow as he played on his guitar. He could hear the humble cry as the man silently prayed while playing the tune of his heart. The angel stared at the window for a long time listening to the man play, readying himself for the task at hand, for like so many prayers, the answer of one was the answer of many.

His eyes scan the building like a soldier taking in the battlefield. He could feel the heavy hearts of the wounded ones, the scarred ones, the tired ones, the hopeful ones, the forgotten ones.

It was a nursing home for Alzheimer's patients.

CORINA ZURCHER & MARYANN BECKMAN

He sighs deeply, "You didn't give me a lot of time on this one." It was the first week of Advent, and expectations and hopes were high on this particular assignment. The angel shakes his head, smiling at the trust his commander, the archangel Gabriel, had for him in accomplishing this mission. "This…is going to take a lot of work." He looks up to the heavens, "I may need a little leeway on this one." He nods and smiles widely, satisfied by the silent reply. "Much appreciated."

The angel heads toward the front doors. He almost reaches the entrance when a young woman comes bursting outside. She breezes past him, heading towards her car. She quickly gets inside, trying to keep her body warm through her thin coat. But instead of starting her car to get the heater going, she sits there in silence, looking completely exhausted. She closes her eyes and takes long, deep breaths, as if this single act and this single moment were all the silence and privacy she would receive the rest of the day. After a few more breaths, she opens her eyes and starts the car—nothing happens. She turns the ignition again. Still nothing. An exasperated look of "I can't believe this" spreads across her face. She turns the ignition once again.

Only a loud whir replies.

She drops her head against the steering wheel, "Really?"

It is then that she hears a light knock on her window. She lifts her head and sees the handsome angel smiling down at her.

"It sounds like a dying cat."

She cannot help but smile in reply. She slowly rolls down her window. "Please tell me you're a mechanic."

"I'm not a mechanic, but I have been known to perform a miracle or two in my time."

"Well, I could use some of your magic. I need to pick up my son from hockey practice."

The angel steps back from her door. "May I?"

"Please do."

She opens the door and steps outside. The angel steps in the driver seat and turns the ignition. The car immediately starts. She shakes her head as a smile of relief spreads across her face. "I knew that was going to happen."

"Ah, yes, the great irony of life, Rebecca." He steps outside. "It seems your car has eight lives left."

"How did you know my name?"

"It's on your name badge."

She looks down at her nurse's uniform and smiles. "Oh!" She laughs.

"My name is Ray."

He extends his hand to her.

"Well, thank you, Ray. I hope some of your magic rubs off on me in case I can't get this thing started tomorrow."

Rebecca climbs back into her car.

"I have a feeling that won't be a problem. But when it comes to problems, never hesitate to ask for help. You'd be surprised at how often people are willing to give it. Have a good evening."

"You too."

Rebecca looks at him with a grateful smile as he helps her shut her door. She drives off while Ray watches her go. He knew all about Rebecca Nicholson—and her entire family.

Ah, yes...the answer of one prayer will be the answer of many.

Ray turns his attention back toward the nursing home and walks down the path to the entrance. As he does, the barren trees suddenly light up one by one as he walks past them. The doors to the nursing home open. He strolls inside.

II

"This coffee has no flavor."

"That's because it's not coffee. It's brown water."

Brett Nicholson, a handsome man in his mid-thirties, is taking a rare coffee break with his co-worker, Stan. Their cubicles are draped with frayed, shiny garland of silver, red and gold. Photos of their family crowd their tiny desk spaces, while heaps of files dominate the remaining space as they tackle the year-end accounting paperwork. Brett sets his Styrofoam cup down with a look of distaste. Better yet, he tosses it in the trash.

"Stan, I don't know how you guys do it. Rebecca and I haven't taken the kids anywhere during their Christmas break...*ever.*"

"Patty's parents help us out or we'd never be able to do it either. Especially since neither of us has had a raise in what..."

"Two years."

"I thought it was four."

"It feels like four."

The door to the conference room opens. Three employees walk out with distraught looks on their faces. The department manager, Mr. Armstrong, waves a few more employees inside. Brett and Stan catch the serious look on their manager's face just as the conference room doors close.

"Hey, Stan, not to sound dismal, but have you noticed lately how the vibe in management's been a little weird?"

"Yeah. Noticing it. You don't think they'd fire anybody before the holidays?"

"End of the quarter, end of the year...it's technically the perfect time to lay people off."

Stan looks at the piles of paper on his desk. "But this is our busiest time of year!"

"When has that ever stopped a company from saving a dime?"

Brett stands and walks over to one of the employees that just left the conference room. Stan follows as they approach another co-worker cleaning out her desk.

"Hey, Linda, is everything okay?"

She stops cleaning and grips her desk. "No." She looks at Stan and Brett. "They just let me go. They're letting a lot of us go. I guess the company's taken more of a hit than they'd like. I was pretty low on the seniority list."

Brett could feel his stomach drop into his feet.

Stan's face turns pale, "Did they say how many they're letting go?"

Linda shakes her head. "They gave me a severance package—a small one, but at least it was something. I just don't know how long it's going to last me. Nobody's hiring in this economy." She starts to cry. "And right before the holidays..."

Looking at Linda putting her family photos inside the small box, Brett suddenly began to think of his own children—all three of them—Gabby, Zach and Beth. He could feel his palms begin to sweat. He could *not* lose his job right now. He and his wife, Rebecca, were struggling enough as it was trying to stay afloat as the cost of living continued to rise, and no raise along with it. Linda was right. The economy was bad. Snow Falls was a small town—a very small town with little room for expanding opportunity—let alone a career change right before Christmas. Losing his job was not an option he could afford to entertain. Just thinking about it made his insides turn.

Standing beside Linda, he could not help but begin to make a mental list—what he did for the company, how many accounts he had, bullet points of his strengths—just in case there was a means to plead for his job. Seeing the tears stream down his co-worker's face, he suddenly kicked himself for thinking only of his own situation when there was someone right in front of him dealing with her own.

Brett touches her shoulder. "I'm sorry, Linda."

Linda gently taps his hand and goes back to cleaning her desk. "Don't be sorry, Brett, you had nothing to do with it. I just hope it works out for you two."

The conference room door opened. More employees exit marked with the same distraught looks on their faces as the group before. Mr. Armstrong peers his head around the doorframe. He sees Stan and Brett. "Brett. Stan. You got a minute?"

Stan doesn't say a word. Brett reluctantly answers, "Sure." He could feel his heart hammering in his chest. *Please, Lord, please let them keep me.*

Linda gives them a sympathetic look as they head inside the conference room.

*   *   *

Zach Nicholson, Brett's athletic ten-year-old son, zooms across the ice. He wears his favorite jersey branded "BANANSKI" on the back in honor of Charlie Bananski, his favorite player. Like a master Stanley Cup champion, he weaves in and out of the other players and drives the puck toward the goal. He shoots...*SCORE!*

Coach Jerry, a forty-two year-old man with a balding head and large potbelly, applauds as the rest of the team skates toward the sidelines.

"Nice work, Nicholson. The Blades are in for it. Final game boys, and you're lookin' good."

David, the coach's son, whispers to Zach as his dad continues his pep talk, "My dad takes winter hockey just as serious as the actual season. He has charts all over the house. It's driving my mom crazy because she can't put up her Christmas decorations."

Zach smiles.

Coach Jerry interrupts, "All right, be on the ice Thursday by five."

The boys head off the ice. Zach and David take the bench and unlace their skates. "You need a ride home?"

"My dad's pickin' me up. Thanks, though."

Stevie, a smaller-sized boy, approaches Zach. His practice clothes are faded and hang on his petite, thin frame. "Hey, Zach?"

"What's up, Stevie?"

Stevie looks down shyly. "Um, is it true that your dad knows Charlie Bananski?"

"Yeah, he grew up with him. Why?"

"Well, I wanted to get my little brother somethin' for Christmas. I thought maybe your dad could ask Mr. Bananski if he would sign my hockey stick for him." Stevie extends his stick to Zach.

David is flabbergasted, "But that's your gaming stick!"

Stevie lowers his head. "Well, I never get to play much anyway. And coach'll never put me in our last game. My brother really likes hockey. More than me."

Zach pauses, "Tell you what, I have an extra stick at home. I'll see if he can sign that one."

A bright smile spreads onto Stevie's face. "Thanks, Zach! See ya Thursday." He races up the snow toward the parking lot with a newfound bounce in his step.

"He was gonna give his stick away? If I had a younger brother, I'd never do that. Especially if that was my only one." David shakes his head.

"My mom said Stevie's family doesn't have much money anymore. Not since his dad died of cancer."

David stops unlacing and looks toward the parking lot and watches as Stevie's mini-van pulls away.

"Yeah...I guess I forgot. That's pretty cool of you to give up your stick."

Zach shrugs it off like it is no big deal. David changes the subject to a lighter topic, "Hey, I didn't know your dad knew Charlie

Bananski!"

"Yeah, they were best friends when they were kids."

"That how you're so good at hockey? Because of your dad?"

"Heck, no! My dad is the worst hockey player ever!"

David looks at him with a confused look on his face. "Then how come you're so good?"

They both stand and head toward the parking lot.

"Because I practice. My dad told me just because you want something, doesn't mean you're going to get it."

"You mean, like being a good hockey player?"

"Yeah, something like that. Anyway, he told me that in order to be good at something and succeed, I needed to work at it. He said, 'Talented people are always practicing their skill even if we don't see them do it; that's why it always looks so easy to the rest of us. Singers are always singing. Dancers are always dancing. They don't just show up on game day hoping to be picked'."

"Hey, that's right. Nobody ever picked me. That's why my dad's the coach. It's the only way I get to play."

Zach looks all around the almost-empty parking lot. Coach Jerry drives over to the boys and rolls down the window. "Hey, Zach, you need a ride?"

"I might. Let me call my mom real quick."

*   *   *

Several black and white photos cover the cream-colored walls inside the small room—most are of old Hollywood movie stars, others are film stills from a golden age gone by. Rebecca tends to her favorite patient, Gertie, a sweet eighty-three-year-old woman with the vibrant eyes of youth. She could not help but chuckle at the picture of the grey-haired woman flipping through an old *Look Magazine* with her hair styled like a teenager from the 1940's.

Gertie looks up and grins, "So...what do you think of my 'do'? I tried to copy it from the magazine."

Rebecca comes closer and examines her hairstyle. Considering how feeble her fingers had become, Gertie had actually done a good job. "Very nice, Gertie."

Gertie beams. "It's for the concert. I just about died when I saw him in *Anchors Away*, but to see him in a real live concert! I'm just so excited. I hope my parents let me go. They should. I'm almost eighteen!"

Her voice was so full of excitement, it made Rebecca want to kick off her shoes and sit down and talk with Gertie all day—like she used to do when she and her girlfriends were young. Come to think of it, she wanted to kick off her shoes anyway. Her feet were killing her. "I think they'll let you go. If not, I'll talk to them. Don't worry."

Gertie smiled at her gratefully and went back to her magazine. Looking at the elderly woman humming in teenage bliss, Rebecca began to wonder. She saw other patients who were angry, some who were sullen and distant, while there were others like Gertie who were filled with childlike joy. Gertie saw everything through the sweet light of an innocent teenager. She saw everything still full of possibilities. Nothing saddened her. When she heard a song she particularly liked, her eyes would fill with a nostalgic glee. It was moments like this where Rebecca felt like she was seeing Gertie as she really was— young at heart.

But why was this age the one Gertie lived in and not any other after? Was this her favorite time of life? Was this the joy she yearned for as she aged year after year before she was diagnosed with Alzheimer's? When Rebecca was a child, her mother would warn her when she made funny faces that her face would "freeze like that"— *beware*. Did Alzheimer's patients' personalities somehow freeze before their mind became totally frozen in the black hole of dementia? It was not a scientific fact or anything they taught in nursing school, but it was something Rebecca wondered about from time to time the more she spent with her patients—especially with ones like Gertie.

Surprisingly, the nursing home gave her a lot of time to think. She was always busy, but in the moments when she was feeding a patient that was unresponsive or helping a patient take a walk around the facility, she would think about her own life as well as the ones under her care.

Rebecca saw the difficulties Alzheimer's brought to the patients and their families all the time. There was Sarah Bielski, formerly Bananski, who would come to visit her mother Agnes almost every day. Sarah would come faithfully to tell her mother stories of the past and fill her in on events of the present while doing something as simple as brushing her mother's hair. Hearing her speak lovingly to an unresponsive mother who did nothing but stare at the walls all day, was painfully beautiful. Her job allowed her to value the moments of everyday life, cherishing every minute with her beloved family—and for that, she was thankful.

Gertie's giggles bring her back to the present as she flips to another page and looks at Rebecca. "Who's your favorite?"

Rebecca thinks hard for Gertie's sake. "Oh, I don't know, it's so hard to pick."

"But if you *had* to choose, who would you pick? Don't pick Frankie! He's mine."

Of course "Frankie" was hers. She probably felt the same way about Brad Pitt back in the day when her and her girlfriends flipped through their *BOP!* and *YM* magazines.

"Hmmm...then I'd have to pick Gene Kelley."

"Yes! That's fantastic! Oh, Mary Beth, we just have to go to the concert together."

Rebecca covers her name badge with her file. There was no need to correct Gertie. Mary Beth was as good a name as any.

"Sounds great, Gertie. See you in a bit."

Rebecca walks back the nurse's station. Her feet were throbbing viciously, reminding her that it had been a long day. All she could think about was how strong her desire was to sit down. But she knew the moment she did, she would not be getting up again. Her best friend, Bess, was typing patient information into the computer from behind the massive counter. She was an older woman in her mid-fifties, but looked like she was in her forties; her dark skin still flawless with age.

Lucky.

"Who'd you pick this time?"

Rebecca writes in Gertie's file. "Gene Kelly, of course."

"I always go with Cary Grant. Soft spot for the handsome ones. Speaking of handsome, have you seen the new orderly? *Mmmhhmmm...*Santa just answered my letter."

Rebecca laughs. "I thought your letter to Santa was for a husband."

Bess laughs deeply. "No, those are my prayers."

As long as Rebecca had known her, Bess had been praying for a husband, lighting candles in church, giving up chocolate for Lent, all in the hopes of one day meeting the man she was destined to spend the rest of her life with. Knowing how much love Bess showered upon her and her children, Rebecca knew if she ever met that man, he would be the luckiest man alive. For now, though, Bess poured out her love as an honorary aunt to Rebecca's three beautiful children.

"Haven't you ever heard that the man of your dreams will come along when you least expect it?"

Bess stops typing and looks at Rebecca, "That's old school. Don't you know you're supposed to pray with expectancy?"

Rebecca smiles. "No, I hadn't heard that. So...is there a deadline on this expectancy?"

"Sooner than later."

Rebecca laughs.

"Besides, that's not how it happened for you."

"Well, no..."

"Uh-huh. That's right. And why is that?"

Rebecca begrudgingly hides a smile.

"I don't hear you."

"Because...I knew..."

"You knew what?"

Rebecca smiles, "All right, I knew I was going to marry him."

"You *expected* to marry him...and you did. Uh-huh."

15

Bess goes back to typing.

Bess was right. Who was she to judge another person's prayer and desire? Not to mention the fact that Bess was right about another thing—Rebecca *had* expected to be Mrs. Brett Nicholson one day. She had known from the time she was seven-years-old that he was the one for her. Not that her sole goal in life was to be married, or that she understood what it meant to find her soul mate at seven, but she had always seemed to know it would be him.

And even as she grew older, she only ever had eyes for Brett…Ryan…Nicholson. Sure, she had dated a little in high school, but nothing serious. Brett never really paid attention to her either— not until Charlie Bananski, his best friend, had asked her out their senior year of high school. That seemed to be what did it. That was the moment he realized she existed, finally asking her if she was serious about Charlie.

It was the moment she had been waiting for. Part of her thought it was the perfect opportunity to blow him off the way he had been doing to her over the years, while another part of her enjoyed seeing him finally take notice—even if it was out of jealousy. Things with Charlie were not serious at all, but Rebecca considered the idea of letting Brett think so—for about a split second. She had waited so long for this shy, quiet boy who had been raised by his grandparents and single mom to approach her one day, that she knew it was a moment to cherish and grasp—not toy with and play games with. They had been together ever since. Even after all these years together, she still cherished every day she spent with Brett. He could still make her heart sing.

Her phone vibrates inside her uniform pocket—it was Zach.

"Hey, how was practice? That's great. No, your dad's picking you up." She looks at her watch and frowns. Bess catches her look. "Okay, tell Coach Jerry thanks. I'll let your dad know. Love you too. Oh! And don't leave your hockey gear in the living room. Your dad tripped over it this morning. All right. See you soon."

"Zach?"

Rebecca nods and checks her text messages. "Brett was supposed to pick him up." She types out a text, yawning as the fatigue sets in. "He's also suppose to pick up the girls."

"You know, I could always take the girls home after my shift. I wouldn't mind watching them until Brett got home."

"No, no, no."

Bess shakes her head and continues typing. Rebecca sees her look. "What?"

"Nothing."

Rebecca yawns again.

Bess stops typing. "What time is it?"

"Quarter to six. Why?"

Bess stands and grabs Rebecca's wrist. "Come on."

"Where are we going?"

"I know you. You haven't taken your break. Don't you know you're required by law to take a ten-minute break, and it's about that time. Besides, you have to see the new orderly." She pulls Rebecca down the hall.

"I only have eyes for my husband."

"Fine by me. All I know is that there's a strappin' young man with the arms of Samson struttin' around here giving this place the kind of life it needs right about now. Besides, I think he's single."

They head down the hall.

III

Brett and Stan exit the conference room and walk in silence back to their cubicle. Several moments pass before either of them speak. Brett looks at the photos of his wife and kids in the corner of his desk.

"I can't believe it."

Stan sits there in disbelief. "I know. They're keeping us."

"But only ten of us. The other thirty were let go—just like that."

Stan looks at the pile of papers on both their desks. He lets out a deep sigh. "I don't know what they're thinking. It's hard enough getting all this work done with a full staff. Now, there's no Christmas bonus. No raise for the next year. Hiring freeze until further notice." Stan sits back in his chair. "Less help, more work. How are we going to get it done? What a nightmare."

Brett attempts to inhale, not realizing how long he seemed to be holding his breath. On the exhale, he allows himself to feel a moment of relief. "At least they kept us." *Thank you, God.* "I don't know what I would've done if they'd fired me. There's nothing else I know how to do."

Stan looks at him and smiles, "What are you talking about? *I* don't know how to do anything else. You write songs and make music."

Brett gives him a look. "I meant for a living, Stan. Dreams and passions don't always pay the bills. At least, it never did for me."

Stan looks at his long-time friend and co-worker with the defeated look on his face just as Mr. Armstrong, their supervisor, walks over.

"I'm going to have Jennifer give you a printout of the account numbers you're taking over so you guys can take a look at them. We need to get all the accounts invoiced before year-end."

They nod in silence as their boss walks away.

Stan lets out a slow breath, "There goes Christmas vacation with the kids. Patty's going have to go without me."

Brett hears his phone vibrating on his desk. He grabs it and sees the text message; he looks at the time on his phone, "Ah, great." He grabs his coat. "I was supposed to pick up Zach from practice, and now I'm late picking up the girls."

"Better get used to it. There's going be a lot more late nights if we're going to get anything done."

Brett grabs a box of files. "I'll work on these at home. See you tomorrow."

Stan nods his goodbye as Brett heads out the door.

*　　*　　*

Bess and Rebecca walk into a large recreation room filled with a few family members visiting with their loved ones. Various patients are also scattered about the room. One patient in particular, Agnes Bananski, sits in a wheelchair in silence, absently looking out the window.

Rebecca sees her twelve-year-old daughter Gabby and eight-year-old daughter Beth and a few other children listening to a handsome man tell them a story. She recognizes him immediately.

"Ray…"

Bess looks at her in surprise. "So you *have* met our new orderly."

"Well, I didn't know he was an orderly at the time. He helped start my car the other night."

"He can start my car any night."

Rebecca ribs Bess. "Stop."

Ray holds a carved, wooden bear in his hand. Beth, Rebecca's youngest daughter, stares at him with rapt attention. Rebecca and Bess listen in.

"Now there's an old Christmas tale where bears like Beth's here..." He nods to Beth; she lowers her head in embarrassment. "Are given a very special gift on Christmas Eve."

The children were spellbound. Even Agnes seemed to be listening from the corner of the room.

"After the clock strikes midnight, all animals around the world are allowed to speak...for one hour."

The children gasp. Gabby's eyes narrow. "Why only an hour on Christmas Eve?"

"It's in honor of Jesus being born."

Beth smiles widely.

"It was the stable animals that surrounded Baby Jesus and kept him company in the manger. They sang to him with all their neighing-melodies of animal lullabies." He looks at the carved bear. "It's God's way of saying thank you to all the animals in the world...for watching over His son."

Beth speaks softly, "I like that story."

Bess and Rebecca stand in the corner behind him. Other family members and patients have turned their attention to Ray as well—he has command of the entire room. Ray hands the bear back to Beth. "Thank you, Beth."

She takes it from him and eyes him curiously, looking all around his head. Ray smiles knowingly, understanding what it is she sees. Gabby, however, narrows her eyes and looks at him skeptically. "I don't believe in fairy tales."

Bess lets out a little "huff." "Listen to that one. Already a little adult."

"Too much of an adult. I wish she weren't so grown up for her age, but that's the way she's always been. She even hated dolls."

Ray looks at Gabby with an amused smile on his face. "Never give up your faith in the old fairy tales, Gabby. They are a pleasant shadow of a lovely truth."

Gabby thinks about this. "I'm going to look that story up on Wikipedia. It never lies."

Ray continues smiling, "Neither do I." He winks at her in a challenge as he stands. Bess and Rebecca walk over to the small group of children.

As soon as Beth sees her mother, she jumps up and dives into Rebecca's legs, "Mommy!"

"Hi, sweetie. You and your sister better get your books. Your dad is on his way."

Gabby stands, "He's late!"

"Yes, I know. Now go grab your things."

Gabby grabs her sister's hand, "C'mon, Beth." They head off to get their backpacks.

Ray turns to Bess and smiles; Bess lets out a low sigh.

"Bess, I meant to tell you that those color scrubs bring out the sparkle in your deep, brown eyes."

Bess beams at Ray, "Why, thank you! I'm always saying that violet is my best color."

Rebecca looks at her in amusement. "Are you blushing?"

Bess nudges her lightly in the ribs. "It's just hot in here. So Ray...I was about to introduce you to one of our best nurses, but it seems you've already met."

Ray turns to Rebecca, "That, we have. How's the car?"

"Purring like a kitten."

He nods over to Gabby and Beth. "Those are your girls, I see. Your oldest is pretty sharp."

Gabby sees them looking at her. She frowns.

"Yes, she is. Her mind is always going. She's like a sponge. She's always trying to figure things out to see how they work."

Beth looks over at Ray. The moment she sees him looking back at her, she looks away shyly.

"And your youngest, Beth..."

"Beth. She's our little miracle. I can still remember when the doctor told us the news, 'Down Syndrome.' He made it sound like the end of the world. At first, we did too, but it's been anything but—it's been a grace."

Bess chuckles, "This whole hospital is filled with little miracles."

The three of them look around the room at all the patients and their families.

Ray nods in agreement, "That's all a person's life really is...a multitude of miracles. If you were to examine each day of every year of your life, you'd see nothing but miracles. Heartache turned to joy, defeat turned to victory, sickness turned to health, hard work coming to fruition, tears of pain turned to laughter."

Bess and Rebecca stare at him.

"And what I love to witness the most are the little miracles you don't see coming. The ones answered off of silent prayers said alone in the dark."

Rebecca replies, "Where did you say you came from?"

Ray smiles. "I'll start taking a few of the patients back to their rooms."

They watch him walk over to Agnes. He says something to her and wheels her out of the room. The other family members and children wave at him as he leaves.

Bess sighs, "That man is a whole bundle of miracles—especially that..."

"Sunshine smile."

Bess chuckles again just as Brett bursts into the recreation room. The moment Rebecca sees him, she glows. Bess smiles to herself and says, "I'm going to get back to the station."

She nods a "hello" to Brett as they pass one another. He rushes over to his wife. "Sorry." He gives Rebecca a quick kiss; she sees the look on his face—she knew all his looks—and this one meant something was wrong.

"What's wrong?"

"They let half the department go."

"What?!?"

"Yeah, I still have my job though."

"Thank God."

Gabby and Beth come in with their backpacks and jackets all ready to go. The moment Beth sees her dad, she breaks out into a run.

"We'll talk about it later."

Beth rushes past a regal-looking patient, Effie, walking down the hallway with the help of her cane. Beth brushes lightly against Effie's long duster, startling the old woman.

Effie shouts at her, "Look where you're going!"

Beth stops and turns around, terrified by the older woman glaring back at her. Effie's face softens the moment she sees Beth's appearance. Beth turns and runs straight toward her parents. Effie straightens out her duster and walks quietly down the hall and back toward her room.

Gabby crosses her arms over her chest as she approaches her dad. "You're late."

Brett smiles at his obstinate daughter, "I thought I'd give you more time to get your homework done."

She shakes her head at him. *"Please."*

Beth runs into his arms. "Daddy!"

He picks her up. "Hi, punkin'."

Rebecca turns to Brett. "Dinner's in the oven. It just needs to be reheated."

Gabby immediately protests, "Oh no! Dad's not allowed to reheat anything."

Brett's eyes grow wide, "Why not?"

"Beth, tell him."

"You burned it the last time, daddy. It tasted like crayon."

Gabby gives her mom a hug and a kiss good-bye. "I got it, mom."

Rebecca gives Brett a quick kiss. "I'll call you later."

Gabby immediately starts talking, "So, dad, today I learned a new acronym. My Dear Aunt Sally. Multiply, divide, add then subtract. Kind of like the planet acronym. But now there's one less planet…"

As they head out the door, Beth sees Ray standing in the doorway.

She peers over Brett's shoulder, staring at Ray. Ray smiles at her the moment he catches her looking. Beth smiles back, seeing the bright glow shining around Ray's head.

IV

Brett trudged up the driveway and into the house with Gabby and Beth. Chipper, the family dog, greets them the moment they walk inside. Guitar music can be heard coming from upstairs. Brett is carrying his box of files from work when he trips over Zach's hockey equipment the moment he walks through the front door. Both Brett and the box fall into the staircase.

"ZACH!"

The music stops. Zach shouts from his room, *"What?!?*

"Get down here and put your equipment away! I'm not going to tell you again!"

Gabby chimes in, "You tell him every day, daddy. You have to hold him accountable or it's never going to work. Come on, Beth." Gabby grabs her sister's hand; they head toward the kitchen as Zach stomps down the stairs.

Brett looks at his unruly son, "Zach, I told you not to leave your stuff around. It's been a long day. The last thing I want to do when I get home is tell you to clean up your mess."

Zach mumbles under his breath, *"Sorr-ree."*

Brett gathers up the spilt files while Zach grabs his gear. Gabby shouts from the kitchen, "Dinner will be ready in fifteen minutes!"

Chipper starts barking.

"Geez! Why's she always yelling?"

"Girls like to yell."

Zach heads up the staircase, "So do dads."

Brett looks up and is about to say something when Gabby and Beth walk back into the living room.

Brett shouts at the dog, "Chipper!"

"Hey, dad, did you hear what I said?"

"Yes, Gabby. The whole house heard you. Take Chipper in the kitchen and feed him, will you?" He gathers up his box and heads down to the basement.

Gabby looks down at the dog and eyes him suspiciously.

Beth tugs at Gabby's apron, "Aren't you gonna take him outside?"

An idea suddenly pops into her head. "Nuh-uh." She points at the dog, "Chipper! Stop barking!"

Chipper stops barking.

"Good boy. Come with me."

Gabby turns and heads down the hall; Chipper and Beth follow.

*   *   *

Brett retreats into his "man cave" carrying the accounting files under his arm. He reaches up and places his hand on a small red guitar mounted on the wall just above a small couch. He speaks forth his wish, "To be one of the great ones." He lets his hand rest against it a little longer than usual, wishing that this ritual bore the result he had longed for rather than the fruitlessness he always faced.

He dumps the box on his desk and takes a deep breath, trying not overwhelm himself with the work he still had to do before the night was over. He could feel his stress level go up a notch just looking at the box. He knew he needed to unwind before he started his work—and there was only one way to do it.

Surrounded by a room filled with country music paraphernalia, he grabs his personal guitar off a stand and begins to play. The strumming calms him little by little as the soft melody fills the small room.

"Thank you, thank you very much...I'd like to dedicate this song to all my fans out there. This is the one that started it all..."

He strums a melody, murmuring the lyrics he began writing long ago. It was a song he had tried to finish time and time again, but never found the exact words that captured its true meaning.

Brett swivels around in his chair and keeps strumming the tune, looking up at the little red instrument as he plays, willing himself to find the words that represented all the things he meant to say.

I was ten-years-old
That Christmas day
When grampa gave me
A little red guitar.
I felt like one of those cowboy stars
Singin' "Home on the Range."

I was twelve-years-old
That Christmas day
When grampa passed on
And rollin' down my face
Were the tears of "Amazing Grace"
That was grampa's favorite song.

Brett plays louder, feeling the words from his heart as he reaches the chorus.

That little red guitar
Is comfort to my heart
In every Christmas song I sing
I feel the warmth that grampa's spirit brings
I'll be strumming out the chords
In honor of our loving Lord
With that little red guitar.

Just outside his office door, Zach listens to his father play. Like so many times before, his father had sung that song. He had never known his Great-grandpa Joe, but he knew his dad loved him and missed him every day—especially at Christmas.

He listened quietly as his dad continued strumming the chords, never finishing that last verse. The moment he heard the melody soften, he gently knocked on the door. "Hey, dad?"

"Yeah?"

Zach opens the door and walks inside, looking up at the red guitar mounted on the wall. "Can I ask you something?"

"Sure."

"Do you think you could ask your friend Charlie if he could sign one of my old hockey sticks?"

Brett sets his guitar down. "*Charlie*. I haven't talked to him in a while. He still play for the Razors?"

"Dad, he's your friend."

"I don't follow hockey anymore." Brett reaches for one of the files and starts skimming through it.

"He's retired now. He's the new commentator for the Flames." He waits for an answer. "Dad?"

Brett puts the file down and grabs another. "You're better off asking your mom. Charlie always had a thing for her. I'm sure she can get him to sign it. Either that or she can just ask Sarah." Brett flips through the pages in the file.

"But dad, it's for..."

Brett tosses the folder down and starts rubbing his temples. "Zach, just ask your mom."

Zach lets out a heavy sigh. "Okay." He looks up at the small instrument on the wall again, admiring it. He had always liked the guitar; he had never seen another one like it. "Hey, dad?"

"Yessss?"

"Were you the same age as me when Great-grandpa Joe gave you that guitar?"

Brett turns away from his files and smiles at Zach in welcome surprise. "Yeah, I was. It was a day when I was feeling really low."

"How come?"

Brett tries to laugh it off. "Well, you know the old ice pond near the nursing home?"

Zach nods.

"That's where me and the neighborhood kids would meet during Christmas break to play hockey. Anyway, I had begged Grandpa Joe for this new hockey stick, thinking that it would somehow make me a better player, and that the guys would suddenly pick me to be on their team."

"Did it work?"

"No, it didn't. I sat on the bench the whole time. The guys even picked one of the girls to play instead of me. She didn't have a stick and asked if she could borrow mine."

"Geez."

"Yeah, it was Charlie Bananski's sister, Sarah. That made me feel even worse. Anyway, I came home feeling pretty sorry for myself. I'd decided that I was never going to go back to that ice pond again."

He looks up at an old photo of Grandpa Joe. "But your great-grandpa wouldn't let me give up. He told me that by not going back the next day, I would never get picked—ever. So I went, hoping I'd finally get my chance."

"And what happened?"

"Charlie picked me to be on his team."

Zach's eyes grow wide, "Wow."

"Yeah, he told me to stand next to the goal and when he hit the puck my way, to knock it in."

"Awesome. Did you win?"

"No, we lost. He hit the puck my way all right, but the moment I swung, I knocked it against the goal post and it ricocheted in the opposite direction."

Zach is speechless. "Grandma Olivia said you were bad at hockey, but I didn't know you were *that* bad."

He eyes his son, "Leave it to your grandma to tell the truth."

"So how did you get the red guitar?"

"After the game that day, I was helping Grandpa Joe get some of the Christmas lights down from the attic. That's when he found it. It used to be his. He gave it to me and taught me how to play."

"Like you taught me."

Brett looks at his son and smiles. "Yeah. I heard you playing up there tonight. New song?"

He shrugs. "I guess. I was just messin' around." Zach looks up at his dad, "I'm sorry I left my gear out. I'll make sure I put it upstairs from now on."

"Just leave it in the garage so you don't have to lug it up and down the stairs every day."

Brett turns and grabs a folder from the box.

"Okay." Zach moves toward the door and suddenly stops, remembering why he originally came down. "Oh, yeah! Gabby told me to tell ya, dinner's ready."

"Tell her I'll be up in a minute."

"You better. She's gonna come down and yell at you if you don't." Zach bounds up the stairs, shutting the door behind him.

*   *   *

Gabby and Beth are on the computer watching a YouTube video on Pavlov's dogs.

"Very interesting..."

Chipper sits on the desk viewing the video as well. Beth stares at the computer screen, watching as the dogs salivate every time a bell rings. "Why are we watching this?"

"I've decided something, Beth. I'm going to teach Chipper to talk. And if I can't do it, then I'll know for sure that animals can't talk. It's the only way to know for sure."

Chipper looks at her. He whines and lowers down onto the desk, resting his head on his paws. Beth strokes him sympathetically as

Gabby continues to study the video as Pavlov demonstrates the Bell Technique."

"Ray said they only talk on Christmas Eve."

She looks at Beth in disbelief. "You don't actually believe that story!"

"Ray doesn't lie!"

"You can't believe everything you hear, Beth. Sometimes you have to see it to believe it." She goes back to the video.

"Why do you wanna see it?"

"Cuz I want to believe it!"

Beth looks at Chipper. He licks her face appreciatively.

"Yeah, I want you to believe it too."

*   *   *

Brett did not know how long he had been working on the files, but the moment he heard the stomping of several feet bounding down the stairs, he knew it had been far too long.

The door bursts open and Gabby, Beth and Chipper storm inside.

"Daddy!"

Brett puts his pen down and swivels around in his chair. "I know, I know. I'm sorry, I got carried away."

Gabby carries in a tray of food and sets it down on his desk. Beth carries a napkin in one hand and the wooden bear in the other.

"You know you're supposed to eat in order to give your brain some food." Gabby hands him his fork while Beth tucks his napkin under his shirt, "Here you go, daddy."

"Thank you."

Beth giggles while Gabby stands there with her hands on her hips looking at the pile of paperwork on the desk. "All right. I'll let you get back to your work while I get back to mine."

"I thought you finished your homework."

"I did. This is a side experiment."

Beth blurts out, "She's trying to teach Chipper to talk."

31

Brett looks at her oddly. He takes a bite of his dinner. "Why? You know dogs can't talk."

She sighs deeply, "That's what I thought up until I saw a video of a German Shepherd saying 'I love you'."

Brett stops mid-bite, "Really?"

Gabby nods. "Do we have a bell anywhere?"

"Uh, try your mom's china hutch."

She nods and looks at Chipper. "Let's go."

He barks and follows her out the door. Brett continues eating. Beth continues to stare at him, as if she was debating about asking him something. Brett puts his fork down and opens his arms; Beth climbs up onto his lap. "What's up, punkin'? How was school today?"

"Okay."

"Yeah? Did you learn anything fun?"

She nods her head. "I learned about angels."

"Angels?"

Beth wraps her arms around his neck. "Daddy, do you believe in angels?"

"You bet. I got you...my tiny angel."

Beth giggles again, her laughter always reminded him of the sound of a tiny bell. "No daddy. *Real* angels."

He takes in his daughter's innocent face. "Yes, I do."

"Me too." She smiles widely. "They look like us, huh?"

"Uh-huh."

"What if you can't see their wings? Are they still angels?"

"Yep. They disguise themselves to look like us sometimes so you don't know they're angels."

"How come?"

"So that way they can perform their miracles without being seen."

Beth thinks about this. "Have you ever seen an angel?"

He nods. "I'm looking at one right now."

She buries her head in his neck. "Daddy..."

He kisses the top of her head. "Your dad needs a kiss."

She lifts her head and gives him a butterfly kiss.

"Did you finish eating?"

She nods.

"Okay, time to go brush your teeth. I'll come tuck you in in a bit."

"Okay. Daddy, will you tell me a story too?"

He nods. She jumps off his lap and runs out the door. Brett sees the wooden bear on the desk. He grabs it and leans back against his chair in stunned silence. He whispers out loud, "Where did she find this?"

He turns it over and runs his fingers over the carved initials on the underbelly. They read, "E.R." Brett sits there for a minute, lost in thought. He remembers the moment when he found it. It was the same day Grandpa Joe had given him the red guitar. He had found his mother's chest of treasures filled with old journals and photographs. It was inside that chest that he found the bear. His biological father had made it for her long ago; and it was the only thing she ever kept of his—other than an old photograph. It was one of the few times Brett had ever remembered asking about his real father or anyone giving him any answers.

"What happened to him, grampa?"

"I don't know. He left your mom shortly after that picture was taken, and she hasn't heard from him since."

"Does he know about me? You can tell me. It's okay. I can take it."

He remembers that moment, waiting for Grandpa Joe's answer. He felt a knot in the pit of his stomach even as he remembered it now.

"Yeah, he knows. Life isn't always easy, kiddo. But that doesn't mean it's always got to be hard either. It wasn't easy for your mom when your dad left. Lots of people in town were mean to her, saying mean things about her because she had a baby and wasn't married. But look at her now. She keeps going, no matter what anybody says. She raised you and moved in here with us so she could go to college to get her degree. So she could have a better life for you two. That's not an easy thing to do."

"You're proud of her, huh?"

He remembers the look on Grandpa Joe's face the moment he answered. *"Yeah, I am. And I'm proud of you too...going back out to that ice pond today.*"

"*I missed the goal, though.*"

"*Not the important one. Sometimes the smallest actions make the biggest noise. You showing up on that ice made all the difference in the world. You did something great.*"

Brett breathes in long and deep, remembering what happened after the puck ricocheted across the ice. It had crossed over onto the center of some darkened ice on the other end of the pond. No one was paying attention when Charlie's sister, Sarah, had skated under the Caution tape and past the cones onto the thin ice to get the puck. It was not until they had heard the ice cracking underneath where Sarah stood that anyone realized what was about to happen.

He could still hear Charlie shout the moment his sister fell through the ice, plunging into the freezing water. Everyone was in a panic, dropping their equipment as they dashed toward Sarah. He could still see Charlie lying on his stomach slowly inching his way toward the center while Sarah fought to stay afloat.

"*Give me your hand!*"

She had reached for it, but she was too far away. Charlie tried to move closer, but the ice started snapping all around them. If they did not get off that part of the ice soon, they would all fall in. It was then that Brett had decided to crawl onto the ice beside Charlie—he was the only one still carrying his stick. He was terrified but somehow managed to find the courage to extend the stick out toward Sarah. She had grabbed hold of it and was not about to let go. It took every ounce of strength he and Charlie could muster to pull her up out of the ice.

They had saved her life.

He and Charlie had become friends that day but had lost touch over the years. Strange how that happens sometimes—even when memories like that one ran so deep. That was the main reason he had not readily agreed to get Zach's hockey stick signed. He was more embarrassed to tell his son that it had been years since he had even spoken to Charlie. He did still talk to Sarah, though. Her and

Charlie's mother, Agnes, was a patient over at the nursing home. And every time he ran into Sarah, she still called him her guardian angel.

He laughed faintly at the title. *An angel.* He thought of Beth and how much he felt that way about his own daughter—not that she was a guardian, but that she was a light all her own, bringing his heavy heart a little bit of light—especially when he needed it most—like tonight.

"My tiny angel..."

He suddenly gets an idea. He sets the bear down and grabs a sheet of paper. He writes rapidly, trying to keep his hand going as fast as the idea had come. Words come pouring out of him as he writes another song. Satisfied with the lyrics, he grabs his guitar and starts strumming another tune in honor of his beloved angel, Beth.

> *I tuck her in on Christmas Eve*
> *A kiss, a prayer before she sleeps*
> *One last hug, turn out the lights*
> *And out of the darkness a voice so sweet*
> *"Daddy, tell me a story before you leave."*
>
> *Snowflakes are falling like tiny angels*
> *And their voices are singing a joyful noel*
> *Silver bells are ringing a heavenly sound...*
>
> *In honor of the baby who would be crowned*
> *The magic of Christmas time is here*
> *For all God's children to embrace and share...*

Brett breathes deeply finishing the song he titles *Tiny Angels*. Setting his guitar down, he is suddenly filled with peace. He picks up another file, feeling rejuvenated in his soul, and works all through the night.

V

Rebecca carries a tray of medication down the hall. She can hear an old woman shouting from inside one of the rooms. Rebecca stops a few feet from the room where the yelling is coming from. Bess comes out carrying a dinner tray, utterly exasperated. "That woman! I swear she's going to be the death of me."

"Are you all right?"

"I'm fine. Miss Effie's just having one of her fits."

They hear the sound of a guitar coming from the room next to Effie's. The old woman shouts again, *"Tell that man to stop playing!!!"* She pounds on the wall with her cane. The music suddenly stops just as Ray comes down the hall carrying another dinner tray.

"Everything all right, ladies? I couldn't help hear all the yelling."

Bess sighs, "Hurricane Effie's on the rampage. She refuses to eat her dinner. Said it has too many vegetables."

They look at the plate filled with soft food.

"I see…"

"Yesterday I brought her vanilla pudding, she wanted chocolate. Then I bring her chocolate, she suddenly wants vanilla. I wouldn't let her get to me this much if she were actually sick or had Alzheimer's."

Bess looks at Ray, "They couldn't handle her at the other home in town. This is the only one left. I know she's a lonely lady with no one to care for her, but still...there's only so much a person can take."

Rebecca places her hand gently on Bess' shoulder to calm her.

Ray grins widely, "Let me see what I can do." He grabs the chocolate pudding and plastic spoon off of Bess' tray and places it beside the vanilla one on his; he heads toward Effie's room.

Ray enters a luxuriously decorated room. Framed photos of movie stills and newspaper clippings cover the walls—similar to the ones hanging in Gertie's room, but these photos were not just prints—they were real. A coat rack with an old fur resides in the corner. A beautiful throw is draped over the edge of the bed. Effie stands in front of one of the photos leaning against her cane.

Ray peers inside. "Knock, knock."

Effie turns her head and scowls. "Who are you?"

"My name is Ray. I thought you might like some dinner." He walks inside the room.

"I told the other one I wasn't going to eat that slop." She moves away from the wall and sits on a nearby chair. Ray sets the tray down and takes in a few of the movie stills.

"Just because I'm old doesn't mean my taste buds have died." Effie closes her eyes and rubs her temples. She opens her eyes and sees Ray staring in the photos. "What are you looking at?"

"*Solitary*. This was your best film, in my humble opinion."

She looks at him skeptically. "You're far too young to have seen any of my films. People in your generation have no appreciation for the art of acting or movie-making. You have no idea who I am."

"I've seen all your movies, Miss DeCarlo."

Her eyes narrow in a challenge, "If that's so, which scene did you like best?"

Ray grabs the spoons and pudding. He sits on the edge of Effie's bed. "The one where you told Richard you had to stay in Ireland to take care of the farm."

Her face softens a bit. He offers Effie the two different puddings. She points to the chocolate one without answering. Ray opens the lid for her and hands it over. He opens the other one and joins her. He points to the photo of *Solitary* with his spoon. "You should've won the Oscar that year."

She nods her head in agreement as she eats. "If it weren't for that Taylor woman, I would have. My career was never the same after that." Effie eyes him as she eats her pudding. "You could've been in movies. You're easy on the eyes, but I'll bet you already knew that."

Ray grins, "I know no such thing. However..." He stands and takes her empty pudding container along with his and tosses it in the trash. He grabs a cup of water from the tray and hands it to her. She takes it. "I do know that you're luckier than most."

She narrows her eyes at him, "How's that?" She starts rocking in her chair.

Ray nods to her photos, "You remember." He looks at her. "You remember what it's like to imagine, to dream and pretend. And you did it well. There are others who aren't so lucky."

They hear the guitar music coming from the next room, but much softer this time. "Take Mr. Reynolds, for example..."

"You mean that man next door with that infernal racket?"

Ray nods. "Actually, I think he plays rather well. He plays his songs hoping they keep his memories strong. Music is the melody of his soul. Without it, he will soon forget...and he will be lost in a dream you cannot imagine, in a world where there is no pretend."

Ray picks up the tray. "The way I see it, why sit in here staring at walls of what you had, when you can be out there showing what you can give? If you think about it, it's a different way to be remembered...even if you're the only one who knows it."

She stops rocking in her chair, the words hitting home with her.

"You know, there's a woman a few doors down who shares your love of film. Her name is Gertie. I think you'll find she is pleasant company." Ray turns toward the doorway. "It was an honor sharing pudding with you, Miss DeCarlo."

"Effie. Call me Effie."

"Good night, Effie."

He walks out. Effie sets the cup down on the night stand beside her and leans her head against the chair. She suddenly decides to close her eyes and listen to the sound of music coming from the room next door once again. The handsome, young man was right—it wasn't as bad as it seemed.

*   *   *

Empty cubicles fill the office, giving it the feel of a ghost town. Brett and Stan work on their files just as Miriam, another co-worker, walks over with a huge gift basket of baked goods in her arms. She sets it down with a loud thump.

"There are twelve more in the receptionist area."

Brett does not even bother to look up. "Re-gift."

Stan leans over and takes a cookie. "I take it Corporate isn't telling our clients that only two people work here now?"

One of the last receptionists turned Jack-of-all trades, Jennifer, walks over and looks at the gift basket, grabbing a chocolate chip muffin. "Oooo, I thought I smelled muffins."

Miriam shakes her head at the slim-figured Jennifer. "If I could look like you and eat like that…here." She hands her the gift basket. "Take it."

"My pleasure."

Miriam is about to leave when she suddenly turns back around, "Oh Brett, I saw this yesterday and thought of you." She hands him a sales flyer; it was for a computer store. "Stan said you write music. It's a pretty good deal on a music program. It records all of your songs and converts them to MP3's so you can upload them onto websites. You can download it from the manufacturer's website, but that in-store deal is a better move."

"Thanks, Miriam." Brett takes the flyer and looks at the holiday sales price; his eyes bug out of his sockets. "*This* is a deal?"

"For that, it is. I'm the coupon and sales deal *queen*. It's not going to get better than that. And if you're going to sell those songs Stan's told me all about, you're going to need to invest in yourself—even if it seems overpriced."

Stan speaks through a mouthful of cookie, "It's a tax write-off for your songwriting business."

"I'll see you guys later. I'm going to grab a cup of that brown water they call coffee."

"Thanks, Miriam."

"Any time. If you decide to buy it, let me know when you've uploaded one of your songs. I'd love to hear one—and buy it." She walks off.

"You just blushed, Brett. I've never seen you do that."

He tosses the paper onto his desk. "I can't believe you told her about my music."

"Well, you were in a band."

"A long time ago."

"And you still write songs. You never know what can happen if the right song gets into the right hands; you could have a second career. And even if it doesn't get into the right hands, you can still sell them off a bunch of different sites and make some money on the side for extra income." Stan grabs the sales flyer and looks at the advertisement. "Besides, what's the point of writing music if nobody ever gets to hear it?"

"Now you're sounding like my wife."

Stan tosses the flyer back on the desk, "Rebecca's a smart woman."

"I don't know about that. If she was smart, she wouldn't have married me. She could've had any guy in this town she wanted, lived in a bigger house, had nicer things."

"That sounds like a violin you're playing, man. Stick to the guitar."

Brett stares at the sales flyer, considering it. "You ever think about a second career?"

Stan shakes his head. "This is all I ever wanted to do."

"Accounting?"

"I'm all about numbers. Always been good at them." Stan goes back to his file. "By the way, I talked to a few of my old contacts at some of the other firms just outside of town."

Brett puts the flyer aside.

Stan continues, "If this place decides to can us, we have options. It'd be a commute, but at least they're options."

Brett looks at the files on his desk. "Thanks. I appreciate that."

"What are friends for?"

They turn back to their work. All the while, Brett stares at the sales flyer, thinking about all the songs he had written over the years. Maybe he could record them and upload them onto a few sites. And who knows, maybe a few people might actually like them enough to buy them.

Thinking about all the new possibilities, Brett realized something he had not considered in a long time—now that he had available options to succeed, even if it was self-made—buying that music program would mean he had no more reason to complain about not doing it; about not becoming the musician or songwriter he had always wanted to be. He had no reason to say "life got in the way, I have no time to do it, or if I didn't have kids…"

He knew Rebecca would be all for it; she was always supportive of everything he did. He was lucky that way. Brett felt the thrill of excitement building from within the more he thought about this new possibility. It was a feeling he had not had in a long time. If he was able to build a second career doing what he loved, Rebecca would not have to work so hard, picking up extra shifts to help them pay for all the unexpected bills that seemed to pop up every time they seemed to finally get ahead. He could finally start to save for the kids' college tuitions and buy them the things they actually wanted instead of the items that were always on sale or clearance. Maybe they could even take a vacation. Better yet, maybe he could even take his wife on a date.

Brett grabs the sales flyer and tucks it into his coat pocket—a whole new dream taking shape inside the confines of his own mind as he felt the seed of hope rising in his heart as he began to prepare for a new dream in life—just in time for the second week of Advent.

VI

Rebecca was having one of those days when all she wanted to do was cry. One of the floor nurses had called in sick and the nursing home was short a nurse for the night shift and needed her to come in. Brett had called to say that he would be at the office late again. There was no one she could call to pick up the girls and watch them until Brett got home, and Zach had a game that night. She did not know what she was going to do. She tried to keep calm, attempting to figure out how she was going to get all the grocery shopping done, the laundry was lying in heaps, the kids were asking when they were going to decorate the Christmas tree, and she had not even begun her Christmas shopping.

"It's going to be okay," she told herself. "Breathe." But no matter how hard she tried, her breathing remained shallow. She called Coach Jerry and asked if he could bring Zach home. She picked up the girls from school and brought them over to the nursing home, but they could not stay there all night. And Zach was far too young to stay at home by himself till all hours of the night. Brett said he would try and see if he could bring more work home, but he did not have access to all the company files to complete the majority of the work he needed to get done.

"Breathe."

Bess sees her zooming down the halls, going from room to room, checking on all the patients. She mutters under her breath, "Poor child."

"What's the matter?" She turns around, startled to see Ray standing right beside her.

"Rebecca. Poor girl is carrying the weight of the world on her shoulders. Never taking any time for herself. Always doing something for somebody."

"She works very hard."

"Always has. Her husband Brett does too. They just laid off most of the staff at his company. He's been working a lot of late nights. The problem is, Rebecca doesn't share much about what's going on in her personal life—at least when there's problems, I mean. Although we're friends, I hardly know sometimes what's going on until far after it's happened. And she never asks for help. I've offered several times to help with the kids, but she doesn't want to burden me, she says."

"What kind of problems?"

She looks all around the lobby to make sure no one is listening. She lowers her voice and continues on, "Well, I couldn't put my finger on it exactly. Brett is a good man. He really is but he seems so...restless. You know the ones. They just keep looking in the rear view mirror rather than the road ahead. Sometimes I think he doesn't appreciate what he's got in front of him—including his wife. If he did, I don't think she'd be so tired. And she's not just tired physically. I can see it, you know? She's tired in her soul. I think all she needs is just a little bit of attention from her man, reminding her that she is a woman, a young woman, who needs to feel appreciated. She's not a workhorse. I think Brett needs to be reminded of that too. Life has a way of draining you. The trick is not to let it."

"You are quite the inspiration, Bess. You're going to make some man a wonderful wife." He beams at her.

She blushes and chuckles. "Oh, you."

"So what do you think we should do?"

"What? About my husband?"

"No, about Rebecca."

"Oh, I don't know. What are you thinking?"

He looks around the lobby. "Well, I'm thinking that most of the patients will be asleep in about an hour, and I won't have much to do. I'm thinking about taking Rebecca for a walk around the block, so she can get some fresh air. Would that be all right with you?"

"Why, I think that's a splendid idea. You know, there's a coffee shop around the corner that's open all night. They sell doughnuts."

"I'll pick some up."

"Ah, Ray, you're the man! You can get me one of those apple fritter things and a large black coffee. Anything is better than the brown water we got brewing in here."

*   *   *

"Thank you, Ray. I really needed to get out and...*walk*." Rebecca laughs freely as they stroll down the street. It was a beautiful night. The stars were glorious in a town like Snow Falls. Here, you could see every constellation throughout the entire galaxy as every space of sky was covered with stars. Rebecca notices Ray's expression as he looks at them in awe.

She looks up at the midnight sky. "I'd forgotten how beautiful the sky looks at night. I'm usually inside. It's so...beautiful." Tears suddenly stream down her face. Rebecca lowers her head and attempts hold them in, but the more she tries to do so, the faster the tears seem to flow.

Ray's face is one of deep concern. "Are you all right?" He hands her a handkerchief from the pocket of his dark, wool coat.

"Thank you. I'm sorry. I'm not usually this emotional."

"There's no need to apologize, Rebecca. You've been under a lot of stress lately. I cannot imagine how hard it is to be a full-time mom, a full-time nurse, and a full-time wife. You make it look easy. You're doing a great job."

Rebecca's tears suddenly stop as a sudden peace fills her heart at the sound of his words. "Thank you. That's really nice of you to say."

"I never lie. I meant every word." Ray looks up at the stars again. "I don't know how anyone can ever tire of looking at the stars. They really are something."

Rebecca stares at him, seeing the look of peacefulness on his face as he stares up at the night sky. "You know, my husband Brett used to have that same look on his face."

Ray looks at her. "What kind is that?"

"One of peace. Confidence. I haven't seen that look on his face in a long time."

"What's the difference between now and then?"

"Oh, life I suppose. He always wanted to be a songwriter, but when we started having kids…well, I suppose life got in the way of that dream."

"You think that's really what it is?"

"What do you mean?"

"I've known many restless men in my life, and there's one thing I've come to understand…it's always something deeper. It's a void no dream can fill, but a reason not to fill it. A reason to let the void grow and spill over into the things that were never meant to be touched by it. Perhaps, there's something Brett has needed long before he ever met you. Even older than the dream he feels he needs to live now that will never make him feel fully alive even if he did."

Rebecca thinks about what he just said, knowing the truth that lies beneath them. She had always thought the same thing but never dared voiced it for fear of Brett's reaction to it, for she knew it was the root of his pain, that constant need to succeed to prove something to a man he never knew but so desperately wanted to know—his biological father. Over the years, Brett refused to even look for him, telling Rebecca that he was not going to chase a man who never chased after him. But she knew he would have welcomed the opportunity to be chased down—even now, she knew he still wanted to be remembered by the one man he believed had forgotten all about him the moment he abandoned him.

They head inside the coffee shop.

"Hi, Ray."

Ray smiles brightly as he greets the owner of the coffee shop. "How's Rover doing?"

"Hanging in there. The vet said the cold is making his hips act up. Can I get you the usual?"

"Yes, please. And an extra large black coffee with an apple fritter, and an extra hot chocolate with non-fat milk and whipped cream."

"You got it."

"How did you know I was going to order that?"

"Bess told me."

"Oh."

He pays for the coffee. While they wait for their order, they look at the Christmas coffee mugs on display. Rebecca picks one of them up and looks at the price.

"So what are you asking for, for Christmas?"

Rebecca does a double-take. "Me?"

Ray laughs. "Yes, you."

"Oh, well…I don't know. Brett and I don't really get each other presents anymore. We usually just focus on the kids. Besides, I have everything I need."

"I don't recall people making Christmas lists filled with things they need. If there was anything in the world that you really wanted, what would it be?"

Rebecca was at a loss for words. It had been a long time since she had thought of anything for herself. She honestly did not know. But then…there *was* something she had always wanted. She smiled to herself, shaking her head as she placed the coffee mug back on the shelf.

"I knew there was something. What is it?"

"It's silly."

"Tell me."

"I…Brett is always writing songs, you know. He puts a lot of thought, time and emotion into them. But he's never written one for me, to tell me how he feels *about* me. I know he loves me, but knowing that his songs are his passion, I'd like to know that I was a part of that passion in some way too. We don't go out like we used to any more. We don't spend time together as much as I'd like. So, I guess…I'd like him to write a song about me so that I know that he really sees me. He's been so wrapped up in his own mind lately, even before all the lay-offs. And I don't want him just to write a song—I want him to sing it to me…in front of a bunch of people."

"You want him to shout it from the rooftops?"

Rebecca laughs. "Why not? You said I could wish for anything in the world!" She looks down and thinks about what she just revealed—or rather, what she finally admitted. She nods her head, "That would be it." She looks up at Ray. "To have my husband sing to me with words from his heart about how he feels about me. I think I've been needing that from him for a long time."

"I think that's doable."

"Hmm?"

"I think our drinks are ready."

They grab their drinks and head back down the street to the nursing home. The entire time, Rebecca could not help but smile, feeling carefree, absorbing the peacefulness that she had not felt in a very long time.

*   *   *

Brett was bent over his desk, fast asleep, still wearing his work clothes from the night before when Beth bursts through the door.

"Daddy! Grandma's on the phone. She wants to talk to you."
She grabs at his hand to help him up.

"Come *on*, daddy!" She tugs at him.

"Okay, I'm coming." He gets up and follows Beth up the stairs.

Rebecca is on the phone. Gabby sifts through Rebecca's recipe box making a list of ingredients while Zach eats a bowl of cereal.

"Make sure you write down peanut butter cookies."

"Got it. What about oatmeal?"

Zach makes a disgusted look. "As long as you don't put any raisins in them."

Beth drags Brett inside. Rebecca takes in his disheveled appearance. She covers the mouth piece, "You want to talk to your mom or do you want to call her back?"

He extends his hand and takes the phone. "Hey, mom."

"Were you sleeping?"

"Yeah, it's been a little crazy lately. "

"That's what Rebecca was telling me. Well, I don't want to keep you, but I wanted to let you know that I'm not going to be able to make it out for Christmas this year."

Brett pauses upon hearing his mother's news.

"Hello? Brett?"

"I heard you. How come?"

Olivia hesitates. "Well, I met someone. We've been dating for some time. His name is Peter, and he's asked me to spend Christmas with him and his family. I'd really like to go." She waits for Brett's answer.

"The kids will be disappointed."

"I thought I'd come visit you for New Year's instead."

"Just you?"

"Just me."

Brett thinks on his mother's news. "Yeah, that should work. At least, we'd get to see you."

Olivia is silent on the other line. "You know Christmas has always been hard for me too, ever since your grandpa died."

He moves into the living room and sits on one of the stairs. "Yeah, I know. I've been thinking about Grandpa Joe a lot lately. Not just because it's Christmas time."

"Oh?"

"Yeah. Beth found the old carved bear. It reminded me of that last Christmas with Grandpa Joe. Right after I found it in the attic, I asked him if my real father knew about me. He had that old box of grandma's Nativity figurines in his hand. I'll never forget what he said, 'Yeah, he knows.' Then he pulled out the Joseph figurine and said, 'Not everyone can be a Joseph'."

His mother did not answer, but he could tell that she was crying.

"But he was like a Joseph, you know? Taking care of me, raising me with you and grandma. I don't know if it's the lay-offs or seeing that wooden bear or what, but I've been thinking a lot about my real dad too. Who he was. What he was like. What his dreams were. What he became. Not really sure why. It's actually been making me think about where I'm at in life. What I always wanted to be—and that…I never became it."

"And what does Rebecca have to say about it?"

"We haven't really seen each other much these last few weeks. We've been so busy working nights."

"So she doesn't know you've been feeling this way?"

"What could she really say about it anyway? My father never wanted me. He never tried to find me. And Grandpa Joe died when I needed him most. There's nothing anybody could say about that— not even Rebecca."

Pouring his heart out to his mother, Brett felt like he could breathe a little bit easier. It was not that he did not want to tell Rebecca how he felt, it's just that there was nothing she could say that would make him feel any better. There was nothing he knew his mother could say either, but he needed to tell someone, and his mother was the only one to tell because she was there at the times he felt the brunt of the loss. They were the men in his life she shared too.

Thinking about how he had just carried on about the two people she had loved and no longer had in her life, he suddenly felt very selfish. She had not called to talk about the past. She had called because she was moving forward into a new kind of future.

"I'm glad you met someone, mom. It's about time you did."

"Thank you, honey. Peter is a wonderful man. I think you're going to like him. But I also think that what you're feeling right now is perfectly normal, but I also think you should tell Rebecca."

Leave it to his mother to assure him he was normal. After she had moved back home at seventeen, pregnant and unmarried, she had gone back to school and gotten her degree in psychology. She continued on while he was growing up, getting her PhD in Clinical Psychology. She was extremely successful, never looking back but forever forward, always telling Brett that life was too short to let pain strip you of the joy you were meant to have in life.

Brett needed that reminder—now more than ever. Telling his mother that he had not even shared his thoughts lately with Rebecca, his best friend, made him feel even more foolish. But for some reason, he simply could not help it. He needed to feel a little bit foolish and a little bit selfish now and then or he would go insane with all the self-sacrifice he felt he had been giving to his family to make ends meet.

Gabby emerges from the kitchen with notepad in hand. "I need to ask grandma what kind of cookies she wants us to make her."

"Hold on, mom. Grandma's not coming this year."

Gabby's jaw drops. "What! But she *has* to come." She shouts toward the kitchen. "Mom! Grandma's not coming for Christmas!"

Zach bursts forth from the kitchen followed by Beth and Rebecca, "Whaddayamean grandma's not coming!"

Olivia closes her eyes as she listens to her grandchildren's retorts over the phone line. Olivia chides her son, "Great. Now you've done it."

"No, you did it by not coming. They want to talk to you. I'm putting you on speaker."

"All right." She takes a deep breath and braces herself. "Hello, everyone."

Gabby jumps right in, "Grandma! Why aren't you coming? I'm making you cookies today. It's tradition!"

Zach jumps in, "Yeah, grandma, what gives?"

Chipper barks in the background.

Brett goads her, "Even Chipper's upset."

Brett, Rebecca and the kids surround the phone. Rebecca looks at

Brett for an answer. He mouths the words, "She met a guy."

Rebecca's eyes grow wide.

"Well, kids, I told your dad I'd be there for New Year's. So I expect double-chocolate chip cookies when I come to visit."

Gabby stands with her hands on her hips, "You still didn't answer the question, grandma."

Rebecca replies, "We'll let grandma tell us when she comes to visit."

Zach turns to Gabby. "You still better make the double-chocolate chip."

"I'm already making you peanut butter and oatmeal."

"So?"

Olivia bursts into laughter.

Beth leans into the phone, "What's so funny, gramma?"

"Oh, I was just thinking about this song your dad wrote when he was a kid. It's the one we used to sing whenever we baked cookies. Brett, do you remember? The one on Christmas recipes. Oh, how did it go..."

Rebecca looks at Brett, "You wrote a song for your mom?"

"Of course. She's my mom."

Olivia continues, "Brett, do you remember...something like, *It's a Christmas recipe...a family thing...*"

The kids look at him, waiting for him to start singing.

"I don't know what your grandma's talking about. She's making up stories again."

"Brett Ryan Nicholson! You know very well you wrote that song. It was your favorite one." She starts singing, "*It's a Christmas recipe...it's a family thing...*"

Brett leans into the phone and starts singing the lyrics, "*It's a Christmas recipe, Handed down from our family tree. You start with a touch of joy to share.*"

Olivia laughs, "That's it!"

Brett and Olivia sing the song together.

"Mix in a pinch of the season's cheer
Add a little wish for peace on earth."

Brett's children laugh in amusement; it has been a long time since they have seen their dad break free in song. Zach looks at him in awe.

They continue singing together, *"Blend in a precious virgin birth."*

Brett wraps his arms around Rebecca and dances around the kitchen with her while Olivia continues singing, *"Sprinkle it with love for the world to see..."*

Brett dips Rebecca as Olivia finishes the song, *"Now you've got a Christmas recipe."*

The kids applaud.

Olivia sighs, "I miss you guys. Have fun baking today. I'll see you soon. Love you."

The kids shout in unison into the phone, "Bye, grandma! Love you!"

Once they hang up, Gabby asks Zach, "Why doesn't she Skype?"

"Old people don't know how to use computers and stuff."

Rebecca turns to Brett, "Think you and Zach can set up the tree while the girls and I bake?"

"Sure." He looks at Gabby. "I want honey jumbles."

She shows him her list. "Got it, dad."

Zach looks at his dad, "You might want to change first. And shower."

Gabby walks up to him and sniffs him. "Yeah, dad, you smell."

"I do?"

Beth giggles. "Like crayons."

VII

Gertie was not in the habit of sneaking into other patient's rooms, but the moment she found out her favorite actress Effie DeCarlo was in the building, she simply could not resist. She had to see her. She was standing in the middle of Effie's room, admiring all the film stills that lined the walls when Effie walked in.

As soon as she saw the female intruder with the 1940's hairdo and *Look Magazine* clutched against her breast, Effie barked louder than normal, "What are you doing in my room?!?"

Gertie jumps, dropping the magazine. Her eyes grow wide the moment she sees the regal figure in front of her. "Oh…my! I can't *believe* it! It *is* you!!!"

She squeals like a teenage girl at a Beatles concert. "I'm Gertie!" She grabs Effie's hand and shakes it up and down.

Effie rips her hand away, "Stop that! You're going to pull by shoulder out of its socket!"

Gertie giggles like a school girl. "Mary Beth is not going to believe it. We just watched your newest film, *Canyon Ridge*. You were soooo good! When Ray told me you lived here, I thought he was just giving me the business. But it's true!!!"

Effie lets out a deep sigh. "Ah, yes…*Ray*."

"Yes! Isn't he dreamy? I swear he should be in movies. I told him he should do a screen test for RKO. He just laughed and laughed."

"I'll bet he did." She moves inside the room and sits down in her favorite rocking chair. "So, you liked *Canyon Ridge?*"

In one seamless motion, Gertie bends down to pick up the magazine and sweeps forward to sit on Effie's bed beside her chair. "*Loved* it."

Gertie looks back at all the film stills on the wall. "You must love being in movies." She looks back at Effie with a curious look. "You look a lot older in person. I'll bet those makeup artists and lighting crews do wonders. I heard they know just how to light all the actresses—like Garbo and Dieterich."

Effie stared at the old woman, listening to the excitement in Gertie's voice, taking in the admiration she could see reflected behind her eyes. It had been a long time since anyone remembered who she was, let alone enjoyed any of her movies. And it had been an even longer time since she had discussed acting or her film career—except for when Ray had entered her room. *Ray.* Part of her wanted to take her cane and whack him over the head with it; she did not like company. She wanted to be left alone. And now, here was this woman, gazing at her in awe, talking passionately about what Effie herself had always loved—*movies.* It was infectious. So much so that Effie found help herself smiling. She answers Gertie's comments with equal enthusiasm. "They did. We would shoot our films in ten or fifteen days. Not like the ones now where they take six months to a year."

Gertie tilts her head to the side and looks at Effie with a confused look on her face. "What do you mean?"

Uh-oh. If Effie was going to engage in conversation with this woman—or any woman—from here on out, she was going to have to remember where she was.

"I meant that the studios are considering changing their ways on how quickly they make their films. Ridiculous, mind you."

Gertie smiles once again and mimics Effie's tone, "Yes, ridiculous!" She giggles again. "Oh! I almost forgot!'

She takes the *Look Magazine* and flips it open. "I was hoping you'd sign this for me."

She hands the magazine to Effie. Effie takes it and finds that it is an old Hollywood photo of her and another actor at the premiere of *Canyon Ridge*. She stares at it for a long time, taking in the days of her youth. She looks up at the old woman and finds Gertie beaming at her. It is then that something inside Effie shifts. She was having a hard time finding her voice, "I would be delighted."

Gertie claps her hands together in glee and giggles. She hands Effie a permanent marker. "Gertie. Make it out to 'My greatest fan, Gertie'."

Effie writes it out and hands it back to Gertie.

"Mary Beth is going to be soooo jealous!"

Gertie pops up from the bed and heads toward the door. She stops and turns back to Effie one last time. "May I come and see you again?"

Effie smiles faintly, "I would like that very much, Gertie."

Gertie jumps up in excitement and practically skips out the door. Effie leans her head against the head rest and begins rocking back and forth. She laughs softly to herself, feeling a little bit more alive, a little bit more important—*remembered*. Just that little bit of attention made her feel significant in a world that no longer cared about whether she lived or died. Ray was right—she was lucky. And not only was she lucky to have had a life that others found to be exciting, but she was lucky to meet someone in a place where everything was forgotten, only to be remembered by someone who held a memory of her—and it was filled with joy.

She hears the faint melody of guitar coming from the next room. Instead of reaching for her cane, Effie closes her eyes and listens to the familiar tune. It was the same melody she always heard him play. She wondered if that was the only one he still remembered, or if it held some sort of significance, perhaps. It really was a pleasant tune—it was the sound of *Amazing Grace*.

*   *   *

Zach and Brett attempt to connect the light cords from one level to the next on the artificial tree. When they finally reach the end, Brett takes the plug and sticks it into the wall socket. "There!"

All levels but one light up. Brett grunts in frustration. Zach looks at the tree and crinkles his nose, "Didn't that happen last year?"

"It happens every year."

Brett pulls the plug out of the socket and begins working on the cords again just as Gabby walks in carrying a few cookies on a bright red plate; Chipper follows closely behind. "Here, you're my taste testers." She hands Brett and Zach a piece of cookie. She turns and takes another piece, holding it out in front of Chipper. She snaps her finger. He immediately sits. She tosses him a piece of cookie. She snaps her fingers again and extends her hand. He puts forth his paw. She hands him another piece of cookie. "Good boy."

Brett and Zach watch in awe. "How'd you get him to do that?"

"I watched a lot of videos on the internet. I couldn't find a bell in mom's china hutch, so I just snap my fingers." She snaps them again. This time she rolls her hand over. Chipper rolls over in reply. She gives him another piece of cookie.

Brett is impressed, "You're pretty good at that."

"Yeah, I know. I'm thinking of working with animals when I grow up. Maybe train some dogs for SEAL Team Six. I saw that on the History Channel."

"I thought you were trying to teach him to talk."

She sighs deeply. "No luck. I think that video I saw was rigged."

Brett attempts to disconnect some of the cords when he asks, "Hey, Gabby, do you know anything about uploading MP3's to websites?"

"I know how to download them, but I'm sure it's pretty simple. Why?"

"Well, I heard that there's this computer program that you can record your songs and then upload them onto a website."

Zach's eyes grow wide, "Cool! Are you going to record some of your songs? Like *Little Red Guitar*?"

"I was thinking about it."

Gabby breathes deeply, "You know, daddy, you're going to have to do more than just upload your songs. You're going to have to get a bunch of Twitter followers and YouTube followers and even a Facebook page."

"All that, huh?"

"That's the only way you can build hype and market yourself for free. But I like the idea. You can record your own album and stop making excuses about not ever doing it. We can talk later." Gabby turns on her heel and heads back into the kitchen. Chipper stays put, obeying the former command. From the kitchen, Gabby snaps her fingers. Chipper turns and runs back into the kitchen.

Brett shakes his head, "That's amazing."

Zach stands there, "But dogs can't talk."

Brett shrugs and goes back to the Christmas lights.

"Hey, dad, when you write a song, what comes first...the words or the melody?" Zach spreads the fake needles on the tree.

"It depends. It works either way for me. Whichever pops into my head first. You thinking about writing a song?"

"Yeah. You think you could teach me?"

"Sure."

Zach smiles from ear to ear. "Cool. I tried writing some stuff down like you do, but I don't really know what I'm doing. Some of the guys from the team want to start a country band."

Brett stops working on the lights and looks at his son. "A band? Really? I was in a band once."

Rebecca walks into the room. "For two weeks. They broke up after one practice."

Brett gives her a look.

"Zach, honey, what time is your game on Thursday?"

"Six, but we have to be there at five." He turns to Brett. "You're gonna be there, right? It's the last game of the season."

Brett plugs the cord into the wall. The bottom level doesn't light up. Brett is lost in his own thoughts.

"Dad?"

"Hmm?"

"My last game..."

"Yeah, I'll be there."

"Promise?"

He answers absently while focusing on the tree, "I promise."

Zach beams and helps his dad go through the rows of lights while Rebecca watches them both; her face is one of hope and concern that Brett would actually find the time to follow through on his promise. She could tell by the look on her son's face that it was one promise Brett needed to keep.

VIII

Rebecca, Gabby and Beth walk inside the nursing home carrying a basket of cookies. Bess sees them coming and immediately rises from behind her desk the moment she sees the large basket. "Are those what I think they are?"

"You bet. The girls and I just dropped some off at the shelter. Of course we had to make a final stop here before Zach's game to share some with the girls' favorite aunt."

Beth grins widely, nodding her head up and down in excitement. "Aunt Bess, I made the ones with pink frosting."

"My, my. You know, pink is my favorite color." She dips her hands inside the basket and grabs a sugar cookie covered in pink frosting.

Gabby narrows her eyes, "I thought it was violet. You said ever since Ray told you they brought out the color of your eyes…"

Rebecca nudges her daughter, "Gabby…."

"What?"

"Shush."

"Mmmm…mmmm…just the way I like them. These are the best pink-colored sugar cookies I've ever had."

Beth giggles in reply.

"Wait till you taste my chocolate chip ones, Aunt Bess."

"I'm looking forward to it, Gabby. I'll just set this basket down right here."

Rebecca looks around the lobby. "Is it me or does this place look different?"

"Oh, so you've noticed."

"Yeah, what is it? It's so quiet in here—peaceful."

Bess bites down into another cookie. "I know. Ever since Ray showed up around here, this place has gone from feeling like a hospital to feeling like home. Even Effie's been easier to deal with. She's even been spending time with Gertie. I walked into her room the other night and they were just sitting there, telling stories—like old girlfriends. Yes, that Ray has done something special around here. He's an angel, I tell you."

Beth gasps.

Gabby looks at her with a questioning look, "What is it, Beth?"

"Aunt Bess said Ray was an angel. *She knows.*"

Bess chuckles in reply, "Well, he is. Speaking of angels, I've finally been able to write out this year's Christmas play, and I want Beth to play the angel."

Gabby burst into laughter. "Whaddayamean 'write out this year's play'? It's the same play every year."

Bess could not help but smile; it was completely true. "All right, so it is. But I did make a few changes...one less shepherd."

Gabby grins.

"Since you know the play so well, why don't you be my assistant director?"

Beth tugs at Rebecca's coat, "What's an asssisss director?"

Gabby turns to her little sister, "It means I get to boss people around."

"But you always boss people around."

"Yeah, well this time I get to do it professionally."

"Oh."

Bess asks Rebecca, "Do you think I can put Zach down to play Joseph?"

"Sure. Sarah will be coming. You can put her kids down too."

"Good. Then I'll fit in the other kids depending on how many show up."

As they continue discussing a few more details on this year's play, Beth turns her head and sees Ray standing in the hallway leaning against one of the doorframes, wearing his long wool coat. He smiles widely the moment their eyes meet.

Beth shyly buries her head against Rebecca's leg. Ray motions for her to come over. She grins from ear to ear and runs over to him without anyone noticing. He crouches down to her so that they are eye to eye. She looks all around his head, seeing the glowing light.

"You see it, don't you? My halo."

She nods her head, "Uh-huh." She leans in closer and cups her tiny hand to his ear; she whispers to him, "Where's your wings?"

Ray looks all around the lobby, making sure no one sees, "I have to hide them so no one can see them."

"How come?"

"Because my wings are really big. I wouldn't be able to walk down the hall if I didn't hide them under my shirt, and I might knock some people over. Besides, I don't want people to know I'm an angel. I'm here to carry out a very secret mission so that I can help someone who is sad be happy."

"Can I help you?"

Ray grins from ear to ear. "As a matter of fact, I think you can. There's someone here who can do a lot of good, if she just came out of her room. I may need you to help me do it."

Beth nods in excitement. She whispers softly once again, "Can I see your wings? I won't tell."

"I'll tell you what…" He reaches up behind his back underneath his shirt. He lifts his hand and pulls out a large ivory feather. He hands it to Beth.

She gasps in awe.

"That makes you an honorary angel. That's my gift to you. And every night before you go to sleep, know that an angel is watching over you, protecting you."

61

Beth whispers to him, "I know. My mom said I have a guarding angel."

Ray laughs softly, "Yes, you do. Do you know why?"

She shakes her head.

"Because God loves you."

Her eyes grow wide. "You know God?"

He nods his head. "I sure do."

"Does that mean you live in heaven?"

"I sure do, and soon I'll be going home. Should we walk back over to your mom and sister?"

She nods her head and grabs his hand, pulling him back over to the nurse's station carrying the ivory feather. She tucks it inside her coat pocket.

"Gabby, I need you and Beth to help me pass out the invitations to the patients. Is Brett coming? He hasn't been here in a long time."

"I'm not sure." Rebecca looks at the time. "We need to get going. I'll see you tomorrow." She turns around and bumps into Ray. "Oh! Ray!

"Well hello, ladies."

"Are you just getting off work?"

"I am. Where are you off to?"

Rebecca is about to answer when Gabby interrupts. "My brother Zach has a hockey game. You wanna come?"

Rebecca laughs nervously, "Gabby, I'm sure Ray has better things to do than go to Zach's game."

"Actually, I don't. I would love to join you. If they win, pizza's on me."

Beth yells, "YAY!!!!"

Gabby grabs Ray's other arm and loops hers through his. "He's coming, mom. Let's go."

Rebecca gives up. "Well, all right then."

Bess takes another cookie from the basket. "Bye-bye. Oh, Ray! If you seen any single gentlemen, send them my way."

"Bess, if I find any gentleman worthy of you—at any time—I will definitely send him your way."

"You're a good man, Ray!"

"Oh!" Gabby stops and runs back to the nurse's station. She leans over and whispers to Bess, "I told dad about dinner with mom. He said to go ahead and make the reservation."

Bess nods and winks at her, "Nice work, little miss. I'll be seeing you soon."

Gabby grins and races back to her mom.

Rebecca questions her, "What did you forget?"

"Nothing! Come on! We're going to be late!"

They head out the door.

*　　*　　*

Zach zooms down the center of the ice weaving past players twice his size. Rebecca, Ray and Beth cheer Zach on from the bleachers while Gabby videotapes the game on Rebecca's phone. "C'mon, Zach!!!"

The entire crowd is on their feet. Only thirty seconds remain in the game; the score is tied 1-1.

Coach Jerry shouts from the sidelines, *"Hook it, Zach!"*

Zach follows his coach's command; he swings. The puck rockets into the net and...*SCORE!!!*

The bleachers erupt like thunder. Gabby takes the phone and videos the crowd. Beth is on top of Ray's shoulders screaming her head off. She turns the phone back to the ice where Zach's teammates surround him, celebrating their victory. Coach Jerry approaches. "That was awesome, Zach!" They hi-five one another. David, Jerry's son, is beside them. "This coming Spring, the season's *ours!"*

Zach is on cloud nine as he looks to the stands. He sees everyone in his family—all except...*dad.* His face suddenly falls. Even from so far back, Rebecca can see the disappointment etched all across Zach's face. It had meant so much to him to have his dad see his last game.

Brett had tried to make it, but all the year-end work they had to do, it was simply going to be impossible. She knew this was going to happen. Not just because Brett had been putting in long hours at work and needed to, but because he had not really been taking an interest in anything outside of whatever he was working on beyond his daily job. And it seemed to be happening more and more.

She heard him at all hours of the night playing his music down in the basement. He had been playing longer than usual, and knowing how much Brett loved music, she knew there was a reason for it. She had even overheard him asking Gabby about the music program the other day while they were putting up the tree. Rebecca was going to ask him about it, but she had wanted to see if he was going to share it with her—like he used to. But he had not said a word. As a matter of fact, he had not said a word to her much about anything at all. It was the first time in her life she felt so distant from him in all the time they had been married—and she did not like it one bit.

Looking at the dejected look on her son's face, she understood how he was feeling. Brett seemed to be in his own world lately, missing out on all the things that were going on all around him. And it was not just about missing a game. He was missing out on life—the life they had both chosen to build on family. Whatever was going on with Brett, it was not just about his job. Ray was right. When it came to men—their motivation was rooted in something more.

Ray turns to Rebecca and sees the distraught look on her face. "That's not the face of a proud mother."

She tries to smile, "I know. It's just that…Brett missed it."

"No, he didn't mom. I taped it on your phone." Gabby hands Rebecca the phone.

A look of relief washes over her face. "Oh, is that what you were doing! I thought you were texting your friends."

"No, no, no…not when it's Zach's last game. It was Ray's idea."

Rebecca looks at him in gratitude. Ray looks at Beth and Gabby. "I don't know about you girls, but I could go for some pepperoni pizza with extra cheese."

Gabby smiles widely, "That's my favorite!"

He grins back at her just as Zach walks up from the ice.

Rebecca leans over and gives him a big hug. "Congratulations, honey!"

Bashfully he replies, "Thanks, mom."

Beth leans over and gives him a hi-five. "Good job, Zach!"

"Thanks, Beth." He looks up at the strange man holding his sister.

Rebecca introduces them, "Zach, this is Ray. He's one of the orderlies over at the nursing home."

"Oh, yeah. Beth and Gabby talk about you a lot."

Gabby blushes. "Do not."

Ray extends his hand in greeting. "Zach, those were some awesome moves down there. You'd give Charlie Bananski a run for his money."

Zach tries to hide his smile. "You like Bananski?"

"He's the greatest hockey player of his generation. He's not even a bad commentator. It takes someone pretty special to have so many talents—kind of like you. I hear you're a pretty good musician."

Gabby rolls her eyes. "He's all right."

Zach narrows his eyes at her. "I'm better than all right. You're just jealous because you don't know how to play."

Rebecca is about to jump in when Ray says, "You know, if you really think about it, we all have different talents. Your mom is an excellent nurse making all her patients feel like family; and she's an amazing mother to you guys—always putting you guys first no matter how tired she is. Being a mom is a hard job—I'll bet she appreciates it every time you say 'thank you'."

The three kids look at their mother; she smiles at them.

"And Zach, you can play sports and write songs. All your experiences, like the one you had today are only going to make you a better songwriter. You're going to be able to write down how you feel about things that other people will be able to understand. Gabby might not be able to play the guitar, but she can figure things out others can't and find new ways to do things. I'm sure her intelligence has helped you out once or twice before."

Zach and Gabby eye one another.

Ray looks up at Beth on his shoulders. "And then there's Beth here who can see things others can't. And I've never met anyone who can make other people smile as much as she can." He looks back down at Zach and Gabby. "Your entire family can do so many things. It's a good thing they're not all the same; it's what makes each of you unique. And who wants to be the same as everybody else?"

Beth yells, "Not me!"

Gabby crosses her arms over her chest and looks at Zach. "All right, you're better than all right."

"Yeah, and I guess you're pretty good about trying to figure out how to teach Chipper to talk."

Rebecca does a double-take, "Wait, what?"

Gabby turns to her mom, "I'll tell you over pizza."

Zach's eyes grow wide, "We're going out for pizza?!?"

Rebecca smiles, "Yep. Ray's buying."

Zach looks up at Ray in awe. "Awesome!"

Ray looks down at Zach, "You know, there's a man at the nursing home—Eric Reynolds—he's a musician too. You should stop in his room and ask him about his songs."

"Cool."

As they head toward the parking lot, Rebecca looks down at her phone and hits "Send."

* * *

Brett is sorting through the files when he gets Rebecca's text. It reads, "THE WINNING GOAL." He sets the paperwork aside and hits "Play." He watches the video of Zach's winning shot. The moment the puck goes through the goalie's legs, a huge smile spreads across Brett's face. He watches the remaining part of the video as the camera pans the crowd. His smile slowly fades the moment he sees the handsome stranger standing beside his wife with his daughter on his shoulders. He plays the video again.

IX

Brett walked inside the house feeling completely drained and exhausted. All he could think about was taking a hot shower and climbing into bed. But the moment he reached the staircase, the idea of climbing up the stairs suddenly depleted any remaining energy he had left. He sees a light coming from the living room.

He walks inside and sees Rebecca on the floor wrapping presents. She looks up at him standing in the entranceway and smiles, "I was wondering if I'd ever see you again."

"Yeah, I'm surprised you're still up."

"I have to work the next few nights, so I figured I'd get some of the wrapping done." She looks up at her husband's tired face. "Did you eat?"

"We ordered takeout."

Rebecca sets the wrapping aside and moves to the couch. "You look like you could use a head rub. Come here." She calls him over to the couch. He takes his jacket off and lays down on Rebecca's lap, using his jacket as a pillow. The moment her fingers touch his temple, Brett could feel his body begin to relax. Rebecca's hands were like magic; he closes his eyes in utter bliss, relishing in her touch.

He breathes deeply. "Thanks for sending that video."

"Zach did a great job. He was so happy."

"Mmm...hmmm..." Any minute now, and Brett would be fast asleep.

"And *my* day? Well, it was pretty busy. We made all the rounds today with the cookies."

His body jerks and his eyes burst open. "You didn't give them all away!"

"No, there's still plenty left in the cookie jar."

He looks at his wife, grinning like a child. Cookies were his weakness. "I meant to ask you about your day. I'm just so tired. And I'm tired of being tired."

"I know."

She continues rubbing his head.

"So who was the guy in the video?"

"What guy?"

"The guy holding Beth."

Rebecca starts laughing. "Oh, that's Ray. He's a new orderly over at the hospital."

He looks up at his wife's smiling face as she replies. He had not seen her smile like that in a long time. He continues to ask her his questions, "So why was he there? Didn't he have anything better to do?"

Rebecca continues smiling, "Apparently not. Gabby invited him to come. He ended up taking us out for pizza afterward."

"He did."

"Yeah. The kids have really taken a liking to him. As a matter of fact, everyone at the hospital adores him—the patients, the staff, all the visitors. I don't know what it is, but he seems to have this gift of bringing out the best in people; he makes you feel good about yourself."

Brett remains utterly silent.

"He's the one who helped start the car a few weeks ago, remember?"

Brett nods his head. He had not remembered, but he was sure to remember the name "Ray" from now on. Hearing his wife talk about another guy, and a good-looking guy from the looks of the video, bothered him. It probably would not have bothered him so much if the guy had stayed at the nursing home to work his wonders there rather than spending time with his family outside of it. *He* was the one who was supposed to be going to his son's game and taking them out for pizza—not some young stud.

Brett crosses his arms over his chest, secretly envying the kind of free time this *Ray* seemed to have, reminding Brett of the time he was used to having. He had decided that when he had kids, he would always make time to do all the things for his children he wished his own father had done—even though he had no father who had ever vowed the same. Realizing that he was not making good on his own promise to himself, the throbbing in his head suddenly returned— and it pounded even harder.

"By the way, the kids' last day of school is tomorrow. I think we can try it out and have them come to the nursing home for a few days. As long as they behave no one should complain. Bess said she could help out and take them home when she got off her shift— since you're probably going to be working late. I don't really like to ask her for help, but if there's no other choice…"

Brett does not reply. Rebecca looks down at him as she strokes his head, trying to interpret his silence. He turns his head and sees a few pieces of paper on the coffee table. He reaches out for them and reads them. "What's this?"

"The kids made their Christmas lists."

He looks at the presents on the ground. "Who are those for?"

"All of our other relatives."

"Mine in there?"

"You're eating yours."

He looks up from the list. "A puppy?"

"Gabby wants to practice her obedience training on another dog."

Brett tosses them on the ground and closes his eyes. He lets out a deep sigh. Rebecca runs her fingers through his hair.

"What's going on with you? And I don't mean about work. There's something else eating at you. Way down here." She points at his heart. He grabs her hand and holds it to his chest. "Is it the news about your mom?"

Several moments pass before he finally speaks. "I've been thinking about a lot of things. It started with the layoffs. I work hard at a job I don't really love, and I almost lost it. It got me thinking about what kind of job would make me happy. And this one...isn't it."

"What do you want to do?"

"I don't know. I feel like I'm spinning my wheels and going nowhere."

"Well, where do you want to go?"

Brett opens his eyes. "That's just it. *I don't know.* I'm just sick of always playing catch up. I wouldn't mind it so much as long as I had a job I was happy doing. It would at least motivate me to keep going, even if I never got ahead. I want to be able to wake up in the morning and be excited to go to work because I'm doing what I'm supposed to be doing. I just don't know exactly what that is."

He closes his eyes once more. He did not want to tell her about how he had been thinking of recording all his songs and selling them on the internet, or that he had been doing research on all the social media sites to help promote them. Brett felt that telling her about it before defining a true motive or goal before then would sound more foolish than anything.

She looks down at his tired face. "All you need is a chance..."

"Hmm?"

"Something you used to say when we were kids. I always wondered what you meant by that. I don't know what made me think of it right at this moment."

Brett lets out a deep sigh.

"I remember it. I wanted the chance to show the world that I mattered. As stupid as it sounds, being picked to play hockey and score a goal was my way of saying, I'm somebody great. I'm worth knowing. I have something to offer."

Rebecca takes in her husband's face as he opens his eyes and stares off in the distance.

"I think I was saying it more to the father I never knew than anybody else. I always wanted him to know what he missed out on by not wanting to know me. I've been thinking a lot about him lately, and I don't know why."

Rebecca waits for him to continue.

"There was this bear that he had given my mother when they were first dating. He had carved it out of his own hands; he even initialed it. Beth had it the other day. I don't even know where she found it. Maybe it was seeing it that triggered it, or maybe it's my mom finally meeting someone, but he's been on my mind ever since—almost as if he was meant to be at this point in my life more than ever. And I know there's nothing to think about except for whatever I used to imagine about him—and I'll never know if I was right or wrong about that. But for some reason, it still matters to me—what he thinks of the boy I was…and the man I am." He grabs Rebecca's hand. "Too bad I just turned out to be average."

She lightly yanks his hair. "Your father, whoever he is, missed out. And you're not average. You're a good father, a wonderful husband…"

"You're biased, Rebecca. Besides, I don't want to just be a good father. I want to be a *great* father, a great husband."

She reaches down and picks up one of the slips of paper from the floor. She puts it on his chest.

"What's this?"

"What *I* want for Christmas."

He reads it. "A song."

"Yeah, you've never written me one, *average* husband of mine. If you can write a song for your mom, you can write at least one for me. Write me a song. Something that tells the world what I've known all along."

"What's that?"

She looks him dead in the eye. "That you're one of the great ones."

He smiles faintly. "Do I have to sing it to you?" A boyish grin spreads across his face. She nods her head.

"In front of a *whole* crowd of people."

He kisses her hand. "I'm going to go to bed." He gets up and heads toward the stairs. Rebecca watches him go. She unfolds his jacket and feels something inside one of the pockets. She pulls out the sales flyer and sees the music program circled in red.

*　　*　　*

Ray walked down the street, heading toward the one spot he came to every evening. He could see the faint glow of the lights leading the way. He stopped the moment he reached the Nativity scene perfectly erected on the snow-covered lawn. He loved coming here night after night taking in the symbolism and constant reminder of the greatest gift of love the world had ever known. God was always sending His love, His help, His mercy and grace—especially when He sent an angel.

Ray looks up at the large angel statue, looking at the enormous wings molded in plaster. There were angels who heralded—like Gabriel. There were warriors like Michael. And there were guardians and messengers—like Ray. He had been sent to Snow Falls in order to bring a message so often heard, yet so rarely believed by the ones who dared to believe it. Miracles of mercy and grace were not just for the faithful—they were for all people—especially the lost and the broken. Most people believed that miracles could happen—but they rarely believed they could actually happen to them. Eric Reynolds was such a man.

Eric had returned to Snow Falls two years before, hoping to one day find and reconnect with the son he had left behind. It was his one regret in life—abandoning what he should have cherished. It was not long after he arrived that he found himself in places he did not remember going. And as time passed, he noticed he was losing his track of the hours and days. He could not recall many of his fondest memories, and names of people he knew and places he had been were lost on him. He knew something was wrong.

The moment he was diagnosed with Alzheimer's, his dreams of reuniting with his son began to fade away—and he was deteriorating fast, faster than most men his age, the doctor said. He moved into the nursing home when he began forgetting his songs and how to play them. Music was his heart, the idol in which he worshipped, and when it began slipping through his fingers, he knew it would not be long before all went dark.

He was not a religious man in any way, but he found himself lying awake at night, staring out his window, talking to the Creator of the universe as he looked up at the stars.

"I'd like to see my son just once and know it was him standing before me. One final memory I can burn into my mind before all my other memories fade away. Please, God…"

It was a powerful prayer. A prayer spoken from the lips of a man who was truly sorry, truly hopeful, truly believing that his prayer just might be answered. But it was a prayer not so easily fulfilled, for there was the son to deal with—even if the son did not want to be. The moment he spoke his prayer out loud, daring to believe that he was actually heard, was the moment Ray was sent to the earth to prove it was so.

All things were possible. It was the son Ray had been working on these last few weeks without even meeting him, for even the son had a prayer he wanted answered—even if he had never spoken it out loud—God had heard it anyway. The father and the son. They were so intertwined. To help the one was to help the other. And it was time to water the seeds Ray had been planting, it was time for them to bloom.

It was the third week of Advent—a time for joy.

A time for joy, indeed.

Ray nods in salute to the angel statue and walks on.

X

"All right, you guys...you ready?"

Zach, Gabby and Beth nod excitedly as they gather up their books and toys. They follow Bess to the nurse's station where they see their mother writing in a patient's file. Another nurse comes through the entrance doors, smiling widely as she sees Bess and the children. Bess winks at her as they head over to Rebecca.

Rebecca looks up and sees her children walking toward her with their coats on. "You heading out now?"

Beth tries not to giggle. Bess answers, "We're *all* heading out right now."

Rebecca looks at her with a confused look on her face. Bess nods to the nurse standing behind Rebecca. Rebecca turns around. "Carol! I didn't know you were coming in tonight."

"Well, I heard you were going out tonight, so I volunteered to take your shift for you."

"Going out?"

Bess grabs Rebecca by the arm. "That's right. You're going out to dinner with that husband of yours. So you need to get home so your girls can help you get dressed."

Rebecca is utterly speechless. Zach hands his mother her coat. "Yeah, mom. Come on!"

Bess squeezes Rebecca's arm, "It's my Christmas present to you."

Rebecca looks at her dear friend in gratitude. "Bess…thank you." She turns to Carol, "And thank you."

Carol beams at her, "It's my pleasure."

"Come on, mom!"

"All right." Zach helps her with her coat. "Brett knows about this?"

Bess nods, "It's all set. He's going to meet you at the restaurant at 7 p.m. sharp! He's coming from work, but he'll be there."

Rebecca's face lights up as she grabs Gabby and Beth's hands. "Well, all right, then let's go!"

Gabby chimes in, "I've already got your dress all picked out."

"You do?"

"Yep, it's the black one you bought last year and have never worn."

Beth looks up at her mother, "I picked out your jooollrey."

"You did?"

She nods excitedly in reply. Rebecca glances back at Bess and mouths, "Thank you."

Bess winks at her. She turns to Zach as they head toward the parking lot, "Now, you take a lesson from me on this. Girls like to get dressed up and taken to fancy places once in a while."

"Who likes girls? *Gross…*"

*   *   *

Rebecca could not remember the last time she and Brett had gone out to dinner, let alone spent any time alone together outside the house. She was still in shock that Bess had even pulled this off, and she was so grateful. Spending a night alone with her husband was exactly what she needed.

The girls had picked out the only black dress she owned. She found it on the clearance rack the year before and tried it on, on a whim. It was a simple, cocktail dress that fit Rebecca perfectly. It showed off her curves in a complimentary way, reminding her that she was not just a mother—but a woman, and a young woman. Beth had picked out her pearl necklace and bracelet that Rebecca's grandmother had given her when she got married.

Seeing her girls get so excited about her getting dressed up to go out, reminded her that it was also important for her children to see this side of her and Brett as well. They were growing up so fast, it would not be long before Gabby and Zach were teenagers. It was important to Rebecca that her daughter know what it was like to be treated with respect by a man, and for her son to know how to treat a woman.

It made Rebecca think about how much her and Brett's love affected their children. It was a thought she never truly comprehended until today. It should not be a rare occasion to go out on a date to spend quality time with your husband. Rebecca was determined that from here on out, she would make a better effort— and share with Brett how much she needed him to make an effort too.

Sitting at the table waiting for Brett to walk through the door, Rebecca felt alive and filled with energy. She felt a sense of peace. Looking around at the warm glow of the restaurant as dimly-lit candles filled the white-linen tables, she felt the love in her heart wanting to burst forth as she thought of Brett, her children and her beloved friends who made this evening possible.

Thank you, God, for tonight. This is such a blessing.

Her phone suddenly starts ringing.

She reaches into her purse and sees that the call is from Brett. "Hi, honey! You almost here?"

The glowing smile on her face suddenly fades. "Oh, I see. There's no other way you can get away?" Tears fill her eyes as the disappointment sets in. She reaches for a Kleenex inside her purse but cannot seem to find one fast enough before the tears start streaming down her face. She tries to keep her voice steady, "I know…all right. Yep, we'll do it another time…bye."

Rebecca quickly clicks off before bursting into tears. She covers her eyes and tries to collect herself as she speaks softly, "It's not a big deal. You can go another night."

She breathes deeply and wipes the remaining tears from her face. She looks around at all the other restaurant patrons dining together trying to decide what to do.

"Rebecca."

She turns to see who called her name, "Ray!" He approaches the table. "What are you doing here?"

"I heard this was the best place to eat. I was about to sit down when I saw you over here. I thought I would come and say hello."

"Well, Brett was supposed to be meeting me for dinner, but he just called to say he won't be able to make it—he's stuck at work."

"That's too bad."

He sees Rebecca's disappointed face.

"Rebecca!"

Rebecca and Ray turn to see Sarah Bielski walking toward them. "I thought that was you." She looks Rebecca up and down. "Look at you! You look absolutely stunning!"

She blushes, "Thank you."

Sarah turns to Ray, "Ray, thank you for suggesting this place to me. I came last night and decided to stop in again. I just came from seeing my mom and thought I'd grab something to eat on the way home. Troy and the kids have already eaten. I often find that I get the best alone-time when I eat by myself before I head home."

"Well, I'm the opposite." Ray pulls a chair out for her. "I hate eating alone. Why don't you and Rebecca join me for dinner? You would both be doing me a great favor by keeping me company."

"I would love to!"

Rebecca nods her head in agreement. "All right."

Sarah sits down beside Rebecca. "Where's my guardian angel this evening?"

"He was supposed to meet me for dinner tonight but has to work late. I just ran into Ray when you came in."

Sarah shakes her head in disapproval, "Well! He's missing out. You look fabulous tonight!"

Ray sits down just as the waiter brings over their menus.

"If I could look like you after having three kids, I'd be happy."

"Sarah, you just made my night." Rebecca smiles widely.

The waiter brings over two more menus. Ray scans the menu while talking, "I saw that Bess put your kids down to be in the play this year."

"Yes, they look forward to it every year." She looks up from the menu. "You know, when I was with my mom today, I was thinking about something, something that I'd really love. I'd like just one more moment where my mom looked at me and knew who I was, so I could tell her I love her. It would mean the world to me. Before her dementia set in, I never got that moment."

Ray replies with, "That's doable."

"What?"

"I know what I'm ordering!" He closes the menu without any further response.

Sarah quickly goes back to scanning hers. She asks, "Speaking of kids, how are Gabby, Zach and Beth?"

They continue their conversation, catching up on their family and friends as the night wears on.

*   *   *

Brett walked into the house and saw Bess and the kids gathered around the television set watching *White Christmas*.

Zach was writing in his notepad, "Hi, dad!"

Beth jumps up and dives into his legs, "Daddy!"

Brett looks over at Bess, "Where's Rebecca?"

Gabby chimes in, "She's still at dinner. She decided to stay."

Brett is taken off-guard be her reply. "It's 10:30! How much longer is she going to be?"

Bess answers, "She didn't say." Without saying another word, Bess stands and heads over to grab her coat. She turns to the kids, "All right, you guys, I'll see you tomorrow." She glances at Brett as she walks out the door, "Good night, Brett."

"Bess."

She stops and looks at him.

"Thanks for doing all this."

"Yeah, I'm sorry it didn't work out." She heads out the door.

Brett turns back into the living room and collapses onto the couch. He reaches for his phone and calls Rebecca—it rings several times before going to voicemail. He decides not to leave her a message. He had worked a long day. He was tired. He was stressed. And seeing that his wife still was not home, eating out at a nice restaurant while he had takeout once again, having the time of her life while he had to come home and put the kids to bed, made him angry. He suddenly felt the pounding in his head.

Chipper began barking at the lights on the tree. "Chipper, stop barking." The dog continues to bark.

Zach moves over beside Brett on the couch, "Hey, dad. When you get to the chorus of a song, how many times should you repeat it?"

"Not now, Zach. Chipper, stop barking."

"I just wanna know. I'm almost done."

"Not now, Zach! Chipper! Stop barking!" He shouted louder than he intended to. Chipper immediately stops.

Gabby and Beth looked at him in silence while Zach's eyes filled with tears, "You promised you were going to teach me how to write a song!"

He closes his eyes and tries to gather his patience. "Zach, I've had a long day." Chipper starts barking at Brett.

"You always say that! You never keep your promises!" Zach jumps off the couch and runs up the stairs, slamming his bedroom door.

Brett looks at Gabby, "Gabby! Would you tell your dog to be quiet!"

Gabby stands and picks up Chipper, holding him close. She looks at her dad; she too has tear-filled eyes. "It's not his fault, daddy. You scared him because you're yelling."

"I'm not yelling!"

Beth stands beside her sister, her eyes are also filled with tears. Gabby moves quickly up the stairs, holding Chipper close. Beth follows her older sister up to their room. The door slams shut behind him.

Great.

Brett grabs his head, resting his elbows on his knees, trying to get his emotions in check. He suddenly hears the front door open. Rebecca walks in humming *Oh Come All Ye Faithful.* She shuts the door behind her and walks into the living room.

"Hi, honey. Did you just get home?"

He does not say a word. She takes off her wool coat and drapes it over a chair. Standing there in her black dress with a huge smile on her face, she looked absolutely radiant. He could feel his stomach drop.

"You wore that?"

Rebecca looks down at her dress. "You like it? The girls helped me get dressed."

"So what took you so long?"

Rebecca hears the tone in his voice. "After I got your call, I was going to come home, but then I ran into Ray and Sarah at the restaurant."

"Ray..."

Brett could feel the hammering inside his head.

"Yes, Ray and Sarah. She's going to get Charlie to sign that hockey stick for Zach's teammate."

But Brett is not listening, "This Ray guy just *happened* to be there."

"They *both* happened to be there. And you would have seen *both* of them had you showed up tonight."

"Well, I had to work tonight while you were out with your friends!"

Rebecca's patience is wearing thin. "You're not the only one who had to work tonight. If Bess hadn't planned this, I'd be at work too!"

"I didn't expect you to stay out all night without me!"

Rebecca shakes her head at him, "So that's what this is about. Say it."

"What."

"You're jealous."

"I am not jealous, Rebecca."

"Yes, you are. You're jealous that I had a nice time tonight, and you're upset that I wasn't home when you got here."

Brett sulks, "Well, you should've been here. You shouldn't have stayed for dinner when it was supposed to be our time together."

"We don't have any 'our time' anymore. That's why tonight meant so much to me. I wanted it to mean just as much to you."

"What do you want me to do? They laid off two-thirds of our company! I can't just up and leave for a night out when everyone else has to stay. It's our busiest time of year. I could lose my job if I didn't put in the same kind of time and energy as everybody else!"

"Then you shouldn't have said 'yes.' You shouldn't have told Bess you would go." Tears start to fill Rebecca's eyes. "Because I was excited, Brett. I was happy tonight. I understand the kind of pressure that you're under, but tonight meant something to me. It reminded me of what I've been missing and needing from you—that I matter."

Brett does not know what to say.

"I know you're unhappy, but the rest of us don't have to be unhappy with you to understand what you're going through." She grabs her coat off the chair. "I needed tonight. I needed to go out and get dressed up and feel pretty. I would've preferred to have spent the evening with you, but I was glad to have spent the evening with friends—even if you aren't happy about it. I love you, honey, but sometimes you can be just a little bit selfish." She turns and walks up the stairs.

The pounding in his head went from a hammer to a drill. He leaned back against the couch and looked at the lights on the Christmas tree. Branch to branch, plug to plug, level to level, the cords had to connect just right in order for the whole tree to light up—a metaphor for his life at the moment. He was out of sync, disconnected from the ones that held him together and brightened up his life, trying to connect on a level that seemed to be the right one but ultimately was the wrong one. It was a matter of figuring out where the plug should ultimately go.

Brett stared at the tree for a long time. It was a beautiful tree. He wanted to be just like it. He wanted his life to twinkle. He wanted it to glow. But sometimes, the best view of the most beautiful things can only be seen when you truly stop and look at them, admiring them for what they are.

Brett headed down the stairs to the basement to sleep on the couch knowing that tonight was where he deserved to go.

XI

Beth and Ray walk down the hall, hand in hand, stopping short just outside of Effie's room. Ray crouches down to Beth. "Now, there's nothing to be afraid of."

"Yes, there is! She yelled at me."

Beth holds a Christmas play invitation in her hand; her carved bear is in the other.

"She yells at everybody."

"Why?"

"Because she's scared."

"Of what?"

"That nobody loves her. We have to show her that just isn't true. And we need Effie. She has a lot of gifts that can help other people here at the hospital. We just need to give her a reason to come outside her room. So I want you to go right on in there and give Miss Effie her invitation."

Beth's eyes grow wide. "You're not comin'?"

"Nope. There are certain messages I'm supposed to give, but this one is for you to give."

Beth still isn't convinced.

"Beth, remember when you asked me why you can't see my wings?"

She nods her head. "You said 'cause you would make people fall over."

Ray laughs. "That's right. But it's also because some people would get really scared if they saw someone like me coming down the hall with great big wings coming out of my back."

Beth giggles.

"So sometimes we need honorary angels like you to help us deliver our messages instead. You think you can help me?"

She nods.

"Good. Now just remember, fear not."

Beth looks at him with a confused look on her face.

"Be...*fearless*."

Beth nods her head slowly in understanding and turns toward the room. Ray watches her go, reminded that this was the final week of Advent—his time on Earth was almost complete and soon he would be leaving. That was the hardest part of an angel's job sometimes, the manner in which you disappeared. Sometimes angels appeared out of nowhere and vanished just as quickly. But when you spent time on the Earth disguised as a human being, vanishing was not so easily done. He had learned, however, that the best thing to do was to slowly remove himself from the picture while bringing in others. This last week he was focused on filling the voids of where he once stood, by filling it with those who would bring friendship and love to those who would need it long after he was gone.

Ray moves to the opposite side of the hallway to wait for Beth. He watches her as she walks inside Effie's room, whispering to herself, "Be fearless."

Rebecca is taking Effie's blood pressure when Beth walks inside. "Hi, honey. What are you doing in here?"

Beth points to Effie and walks over to her. "Miss Effie..."

Effie looks at her curiously, "Yes?"

Beth looks down at the paper in her hand. "Here." She quickly hands Effie the invitation and bolts out of the room. Effie looks down at the tiny piece of green and red paper. She opens it and reads it, reminded of another young girl Effie once knew. "Is that your daughter?"

Rebecca nods. "Her name's Beth. And it looks like she's terrified of you."

"Hmmph." Effie eyes Rebecca as she writes in the file. "Are you sorry you had her?"

Rebecca is taken off-guard by the question but recovers quickly. "No, I'm not."

"It's nice to see her out and about. In my day, they did otherwise. I had a younger sister much like your Beth. She was sent to an institution to live. She died there. She was the sweetest person I ever knew."

Rebecca closes the file and looks at Effie, "People used to ask me that question all the time. And those same people looked at me and felt sorry for me, thinking my daughter must be some kind of burden when she's quite the opposite. She's a miracle."

Effie runs her withered fingers over the invitation. "I've heard it said that there are only two ways to live life: one is as if nothing is a miracle. The other is as though everything is." She looks up at Rebecca. "I can see which path you've chosen. I wish I had chosen the same."

Rebecca softens a bit, "Do you have any children, Effie?"

"No. I was married once to Herbert Walls—an actor. I didn't love him; we just photographed well together."

"What happened to him?"

"Divorced him. He didn't love me either. Eh!"

"That's too bad."

Effie is lost in her memories, "But there was one man I should've married."

"What was his name?"

Effie looks off in the distance. "Freddy Manning. He was a cameraman. Barely finished high school, average-looking I suppose, but he had the sweetest smile...I loved him very much." A pleasant smile forms on her face.

"Did he ever marry?"

"I have no idea. When my contract ended, I moved to another studio. That's when I married Herbert." Thinking about her sister and the love she used to have, she suddenly felt very lonely. Effie shivers and wraps her arms around herself. "It's so cold in here."

Rebecca reaches for Effie's fur coat. "Here." She wraps it around Effie. "I'll let you rest now."

Rebecca heads out the door while Effie rocks silently back and forth. She looks down at the invitation in her hand and suddenly feels a stirring deep within her heart.

*   *   *

Eric Reynolds is sitting in his room listening to Zach give a play by play of his last hockey game while holding an old, acoustic guitar in his hands. Little wooden animals fill the windowsill in the small room, while various photos of Eric in his younger days adorn the walls. Most of them are of him with his band and other musicians, marking his travels all across the world. Little post-its mark the frames, each with names, dates and locations—little reminders to himself of what they are and represent.

"This goalie was a giant! Mom didn't think he was ten, but he must've been because his dad was just as huge!"

"So how'd you get the puck past him?"

"I closed my eyes...and swung."

Eric chuckles. "Well, sometimes that's how things in life get done... you just swing away. Your dad pretty good at hockey?"

"Nah. He's not very coordinated, but he plays the guitar pretty well."

Eric softly strums his guitar. "Well now, that takes a lot of coordination. I wasn't very good at sports myself, but I had a knack for playing instruments—and I loved music.

Zach watches Eric's fingers as they move easily across the board. "That's my dad's favorite tune. He played it at my great-grandpa's funeral when he was a kid."

"Is that right?"

Brett walks down the hall carrying a bouquet of flowers. He had not spoken with Rebecca or the kids in the kids all day, trying to figure out the best way to say he was sorry. Rebecca was right. He had been acting selfish lately. He vowed to be better about meeting his family's needs—especially since he had been so focused on his own. That's always the danger of living your life inside your own head, making your own plans without telling the people they would affect. You end up neglecting the life you are actually living.

As he heads toward the nurse's station, he suddenly notices the change in the nursing home. He could not put his finger on exactly what it was, but it seemed to feel...peaceful.

"Brett, you shouldn't have."

Bess winks at him as he approaches the desk. "Actually, I should." He pulls one of the flowers from the bouquet. "Thank you again, for last night—even though I didn't make good on my promise."

"Ah, now, there are other chances for other days."

Brett smiles faintly, "Not always. Are you watching the kids tonight?"

"No, Rebecca found a babysitter."

"Oh?"

"Sarah's daughter, Jules. I guess they discussed it last night at dinner. I'm proud of Rebecca. She's finally asking for help and looking at it as a good thing."

"Is Rebecca around?"

"She's making the rounds right now, but she'll be by shortly. You on a lunch break?"

"A late lunch break. I thought I'd finally take it and head over here for a minute or two before heading back. It wasn't a great evening after you left."

"Rebecca told me. The girls are in the recreation room rehearsing for the play, but Zach is down the hall in Mr. Reynolds' room if you want to see them before Rebecca gets back."

"Yeah, I think I will. What room is Mr. Reynolds' in?"

"Room 207. You can leave the flowers here until you get back."

"Thanks, Bess." He heads down the hall. The moment he hears the faint melody of *Amazing Grace*, he slows his steps. He hears an older man's voice coming from inside the room.

"Thanks for helping me with this last part. I've been trying to finish it for a while. I asked my dad to help me, but he's been really busy at work."

"Well, that's what father's are for. They work hard to provide for their families. Sometimes they miss out on the day-to-day happenings because of it, like you learning to write a song. I'm sure he would have found the time to help you at some point."

"Yeah, probably."

Brett feels his stomach twist into a tight knot as he listens in on the conversation.

"I'll tell you what, bring your guitar next time and I'll teach you a few more things, help you write some hit songs with that band of yours."

Zach's face brightens. "Cool!"

Brett knocks on the door.

"Dad! What are you doing here?"

"I came by to see your mom on my break."

Eric stops playing and smiles at Brett.

"Mr. Reynolds, this is my dad."

"Call me Eric."

Brett approaches. They shake hands. "Call me Brett."

"It's an honor to meet you, Brett. I've heard a lot about you. This young man here is your greatest admirer."

Zach blushes in embarrassment. "I gotta go to the bathroom. Are you going to be here when I get back?"

"No, I need to get back to work, but I'll see you tonight."

"Okay." Zach heads down the hall, leaving Eric and Brett alone.

"That's a fine boy you got there."

"Thank you, I appreciate that. It's nice to hear he somewhat behaves when I'm not around."

Brett notices the photos on the wall; he reads a few of the post-it notes.

"Ah, what boy isn't rambunctious in some way. Wouldn't seem right if a boy weren't on the hunt for some kind of adventure. I see you like my pictures."

Brett turns back to them, "Yeah, is that..."

"Sure is. Opened for him a few times."

Brett continues to look at all the photos. "Wow."

"Young Zach says you like to play a little too."

He turns back to Eric. "Not as much as I used to or that I'd like. It's become more of a hobby than anything. Maybe someday I can do more with it."

"You sound a little down about that, like you'd like that someday to be today."

Brett pauses. "Is it that obvious?"

Eric chuckles. "Son, you look at these photos and see a dream come to pass. I look at these photos and sometimes wish there were other people in them—like family." He looks at Brett with a sad smile, "You're lucky. I wish I realized how lucky I was when I had the chance."

"You don't have any family?"

"I had a son. Never met him though. Too busy living the dream. I came back here a few years ago, hoping to find him. Wound up here instead."

"Does he still live here?"

"I don't know. But I think about him a lot, wondering what he looks like, what he became. If he's anything like me. Or better yet, if he's the complete opposite."

Brett smiles faintly. "Maybe you could still find him."

Eric shakes his head. "I've left him alone all this time, why bother him now? Especially now...would seem cruel to meet him today and forget him tomorrow, wouldn't it?" He looks to Brett for affirmation.

"I guess it depends on how your son feels about it."

"I guess you're right about that. I suppose that's why I still pray about it—that maybe I'll see him some day. I envy you. You and your boy."

Eric's words resonate deep within Brett's soul. Looking at the older man in front of him, there was something familiar. He was not sure what it was, but it was a feeling he had that he somehow knew this man. Or perhaps it was nothing more than a connection he felt with him over their fondness for music and a similar passion for song. Whatever it was, Brett knew that he liked him. He felt himself hoping that Eric's prayers would be answered, and that he would one day find his son.

Brett glances up and sees the carved wooden animal figurines on the windowsill when Bess pops her head inside the room. "Brett, Rebecca's back from making her rounds."

"Thanks." He looks down at Eric. "Have a good night."

"You too."

As Brett heads into the hallway, Eric begins playing the tune to *Amazing Grace* once more. Hearing the soft melody as he heads back toward the nurse's station to see his wife, Brett suddenly felt a gnawing feeling in the back of his mind. There was something he had missed and he was not sure what it was. But the moment he saw Rebecca holding the bouquet of flowers in her hands smiling back at him, he knew it could not be as important as this.

XII

Later that night, Brett came home to the soft glow of Christmas lights twinkling off the tree in the living room. Presents filled the bottom of it, reminding Brett of the present Rebecca still wanted.

He heads up the stairs and checks in on Zach and the girls. A small lamp was on inside the girls' room. He walks quietly inside to turn it off when he sees a large, white feather on the nightstand beside Beth's bed. He touches it lightly, wondering what kind of bird it must have come from. Right beside the feather is the carved, wooden bear. Brett looks at it, suddenly realizing what it was that bothered him the moment he left Eric Reynolds' room.

The wooden animals.

He turns it over and runs his fingers over the initials carved on the belly—*E.R.* His heart begins to hammer inside his chest. Brett takes the bear off the night stand, turns off the lamp, and heads down to the basement.

He sets the bear down on top of his desk and immediately starts going through the drawers, frantically searching through them.

"It can't be..."

Brett stops the moment he finds what he is looking for. He pulls out an old photo of his mother and his biological father. It was the only photo she ever kept of him, and it was the one he found the same day he found the bear in the attic.

Brett looks at it for a long time, recognizing the face of his father in the days of his youth—it was the same face he had seen on the photos lining the walls in Eric's room.

Brett can barely breathe as the realization that he met his father without even knowing it—and that his father had met *him*.

*　　*　　*

The next morning, Zach ventures into the basement carrying his guitar. He jumps onto the couch and touches the one mounted on the wall. "To be one of the great ones."

He jumps down and sits on the couch, strumming the tune he had been working on. He gets up and moves over to his father's desk. He sifts through some of the papers and sees the stack of songs Brett had written over the years. He pulls out the one entitled *Little Red Guitar*. He smiles brightly, strumming the tune and singing the words, *"I was ten years old that Christmas day, when grampa gave me a little red guitar..."*

The string on Zach's guitar suddenly breaks.

"Man!"

Zach sets his guitar down and grabs Brett's from the stand beside the desk. He picks it up and tries to play the chords but realizes the instrument is too big for him. He sets it back down, grabbing his own guitar. He is about to head back upstairs when he looks up at the little red guitar mounted on the wall.

Zach sets his guitar down and climbs on top of the couch. He reaches for the small instrument, but it is too high for him to lift off the wall. He stands on his tip-toes, barely grabbing hold of the guitar when he loses his balance. He falls backward and lands on the ground—taking the red guitar with him.

Rebecca shouts from upstairs, "Zach??? Everything okay?"

Zach sits up and looks at the instrument. The bridge is dislodged, along with all the strings. Looking at the broken guitar, Zach suddenly panics.

"Yeah!"

He tries to put the bridge back on.

"What am I gonna do?"

Zach picks up the guitar and runs quickly up the stairs.

*   *   *

"Right there, Gabby. Good." Bess and Gabby direct a small group of children for the upcoming Christmas play. Gabby is on stage with the other children while Beth stands beside Bess on the ground floor.

"Now where is Zach?"

"He'll be here. He had to take care of something."

"Well, he should be in here rehearsing."

Beth sees Effie walking toward them; Gertie follows close behind. She grabs onto Bess' uniform and tugs at her. Bess turns and sees Effie, "Oh Lord, give me patience."

Effie looks up at the children on stage. "I heard you were in charge of the Christmas play."

"That's right. We're rehearsing right now."

Effie takes a deep breath and looks at Bess, "Could you use any help? I have some prior experience with such things."

Gertie chimes in, "She's an actress, you know."

"Yes, Gertie, I know."

An awkward silence follows.

"Gabby is our assistant director." Bess looks at Gabby, "What do you think? Could we use Miss DeCarlo's help?"

"Call me Effie."

Gabby cocks her head to the side, contemplating the idea. "All right."

Gertie jumps for joy, "Oh, goodie! I'll just watch." She pulls up a chair and sets it up right in front of the stage.

Gabby jumps off the stage and hands Effie a copy of the play. "We're on the part where the angel walks in. Beth is playing the angel."

Effie spots Beth cowering behind Bess. The moment Beth makes eye contact with Effie, she runs to the other end of the room.

Gabby shouts after her, "Beth!"

Beth runs over to the far corner. Beth crouches down and covers her eyes. Gabby moves to go after her when Effie stops her. "I'll go. You go ahead with the next scene."

Effie makes her way over to Beth. Beth opens and closes her hands attempting to hide from her. Ray, unseen, watches from a distance.

"Beth, may I sit here for a moment? My feet are tired."

Beth opens her hands and peers up at her but remains silent. Effie sits and looks down at Beth, "I've come to say, I'm sorry. I yelled at you some time ago, and I shouldn't have. I didn't mean to scare you." Beth's eyes remain fixed on her. "You scared me too."

"How?"

"When you ran past me, I thought I was going to fall. And that scared me very much." Effie leans in, "Do you think you can forgive me, Beth? I'd like to be friends."

Beth lowers her hands and smiles.

Encouraged, Effie adds, "And I wanted to thank you for the Christmas invitation."

"You're welcome." Beth wraps her arms around Effie's legs and gives her a big hug. Effie looks uncomfortable at first, but then rests her hand on Beth's head; a faint smile forms on Effie's lips. "Oh, you are an angel, aren't you."

Beth looks across the room and sees Ray. He gives her the "thumbs up" sign. Beth grins from ear to ear as Ray heads down the hall.

* * *

Brett decided to go to the nursing home on his lunch break. He had not been able to sleep all night, and he had not been able to work all day. He had not said a word to anyone about Eric. He was still trying to take it all in himself. He had even debated about calling his mother but thought against it, not knowing how she would take the news.

Brett thought the only thing he could do was to go and see his father and tell him who he was. He did not know exactly what he was going to say or how he was going to say it, but he could not function until he did.

Carrying the wooden bear in his hand, he heads inside the nursing home. As he approaches Room 207, he sees Eric standing by one of the windows further down the hall. Brett takes in the distant look on Eric's face and slowly approaches.

"Mr. Reynolds?"

Eric continues to stare out the window. Brett moves closer and touches his arm. "Eric..."

Eric turns his head, but there is no recognition behind his eyes.

"My name is Brett. I met you yesterday. You were spending time with my son, Zach."

Eric remains silent, taking in Brett. He grabs Brett's arm. "I told her I couldn't stay. Olivia..."

Brett swallows hard.

"A wife and a baby? I was going on tour for the first time...she wanted to go with me. That kind of life...it wasn't for me..."

Brett listens intently to what Eric is saying.

"The fans, they just scream your name." He looks Brett dead in the eye. "Great for the moment. For a moment it's amazing. Then it all goes away...it's all so quiet now. So quiet." He stops talking.

Brett can barely breathe. "I'm going to take you back to your room."

They move inside the tiny room. Eric takes in the environment as if it was the first time he had ever seen it. Eric looks up at Brett. "Is it too late to ask him for forgiveness? For leaving him behind?"

Brett swallows hard, "I...I don't know. I guess it depends...on the son."

"My guitar..." The old man reaches for his guitar. Not knowing what to do, Brett gives it to him. Eric tries to play the guitar, but he cannot remember how. He holds the guitar close to his chest and stares out the window.

Bess walks inside. "Brett! I didn't know you were here." She sees the look on his face. "Are you all right?"

Brett dares not look at Eric. "I...I, uh...Bess, Mr. Reynolds is my biological father."

Bess gasps, "My word…"

Brett moves past her, "I need to get out of here."

Bess calls after him, "Brett!" She turns back around and looks at Eric. "My word…"

* * *

Rebecca parks the car and walks toward the bridge that overlooks the old hockey ice pond. She sees Brett standing on the bridge, looking off in the distance. She walks up beside him and touches his hand, looking out at the pond alongside him.

"Bess told me…about Mr. Reynolds."

Brett does not answer but simply nods his head.

Rebecca silently prays that God would give her the right words to say what her husband needed her to say. She lays her hand gently on his arm. "You know, I've never believed in coincidence. I always knew I was going to be a nurse. But to know you would one day meet your father because I became one...I look at this moment and am in awe; it's a blessing, Brett. A chance for you to find peace from what's aching right in here." She points to his heart. "But I need to know how you see this, how you feel about it."

Brett is quiet for a moment. "There's so many things I'm feeling right now...all the ways I imagined this moment, what I'd say to him, what I wouldn't say..." He looks out at the far end of the pond. "I've felt this void all my life, this strange detachment from things that's always had me searching. It was something Grandpa Joe couldn't fill, something my mom never understood. And part of me doesn't want to let go of it." Brett looks at Rebecca. "It's made me who I am, the father I am...searching to find a way to be good at what's in front of me, to be better than the choices that have shaped me. And I didn't realize until now, that it's because of him."

He shakes his head. "And in all my searching, there's a reason I never looked for him, Rebecca. And he found me anyway. I'm not ready for it. I was supposed to..." He struggles with his thoughts.

"What?"

He shakes his head. She holds his arm tighter, giving him silent support.

"What?"

"I was supposed to do something *great. Be* something great before I met him."

Rebecca pulls out the sales flyer from her coat pocket. "Is that what this was all about?"

He clenches his jaw in embarrassment and turns. He starts walking off the bridge.

"Brett..." Brett keeps walking. Rebecca follows behind him. *"Brett! Please don't walk away from me!"*

He finally stops and faces her, grabbing the flyer from her hand. "This was about spinning my wheels. This was about feeling good about myself. For me to be able to say to our kids, 'Follow your dreams. Anything is possible if you work hard and try.' How can I say that when I haven't even done anything myself? I never followed my dream. It's all just words, Rebecca. And I want my example to be my words. Not just for me, but to able to say to *him*, 'You see...'"

"I matter."

Brett looks at his wife, hearing the truth in her words. He lowers his head, "Yeah. I haven't had that feeling since that day out on the ice when I saved Sarah."

He crumples the flyer. "I don't want to need that feeling, but I do. Why I need it now more than any other, I don't know." Brett looks up at the sky. Rebecca takes his hand.

"Maybe because what you're looking for is not what you're

supposed to find." Brett looks at her. "If you had made it as a famous singer, we would be entirely different people. You'd be on the road all the time, away from me and the kids—if we'd even had any kids. You'd be a young Mr. Reynolds. I've seen the pictures on his wall. I've heard his stories."

He holds her stare.

"To be great in the little things, to be truly noble and heroic in the smallest details of everyday life *is* a virtue. Yet you seem to think the little things are average, that only great moments come when everyone can see them. The greatest moments are the ones you don't see coming." She touches his face. "Maybe instead of spinning your wheels, you're supposed to brake. Maybe you're right where you're supposed to be, doing exactly what you're supposed to be doing."

"Searching?"

Rebecca shakes her head. "*Growing.* Write your songs. There's a reason for them, and that reason will one day show its face. Just like you not getting picked to play hockey one day, only to get picked the next." Brett touches his wife's face. "Fill your void, honey. Speak to Mr. Reynolds. He's a nice man. Zach likes him."

Tears fill his eyes. "So do I. I feel like I should hate him. That this rage should be burning deep inside me, but I don't have it."

"That's because you know how to love, Brett. Through all the pain and sorrow you've experienced, you've never been so scarred as to forget how to love. That's why I married you. You're one of the rare ones."

Brett rests his head against hers. "I don't know what I'd do without you."

He kisses her softly on the lips.

She touches his face, "Is that the first line to my song?"

He smiles back at her. "You and that song."

XIII

*I*t was Christmas Eve. Families had gathered together inside the nursing home to visit with their cherished friends and loved ones. It was tradition at the home to host a Christmas dinner early in the evening, followed by the children's play a little later that night.

Rebecca was working the early shift so she could be home with the kids on Christmas Day. While she visited with the visiting families, Gabby and Beth were in the recreation room preparing for the play.

Bess was running around the stage area with her clipboard, checking off all the cast members in attendance. "Where's Zach?!?"

"He's here. He's just visiting with Mr. Reynolds."

"Well, he's supposed to be in here getting dressed!"

Gabby jumps off the stage, "I can go get him."

"No, you stay here and make sure no one else leaves the room. You're in charge. Just make sure everyone is in full costume. We're on in fifteen minutes!" Bess rushes outside the room.

Gabby turns toward the cast, "All right! Places everyone!"

Nobody moves. Seeing the child-like faces before her, Gabby sighs. "Okay, you! Stand here." She starts putting everyone in their places. Ray walks up to the stage and approaches Beth.

"My honorary angel."

Beth smiles widely. He sees the wooden bear in her hand. "May I borrow that, Beth?"

She nods her head and hands it to him.

"Thank you. I'll bring it back."

"Promise?"

"I promise."

* * *

Brett heads inside the nursing home just as Bess rushes past. "Oh, Brett! Would you do me a favor?"

"Sure."

"Find Zach. He's our Joseph and he's supposed to be on stage in fifteen minutes. I think he's in Mr. Reynolds' room."

Brett feels his heart begin to pound. "All right."

"God bless you." She runs off toward the cafeteria.

Brett stands there for a minute, gathering his emotions and collecting his thoughts. *Lord, help me please.* He heads down the hall toward Room 207.

Eric and Zach are gluing the bridge back onto the guitar with wood glue. "There, now this looks worse than what it is. Nothing some good old wood glue can't fix. As soon as this dries, we'll adjust the strings and it'll be as good as new."

Brett approaches Eric's room. What was he going to say? Would Eric remember him this time? He drops his head and exhales, "Just get it over with, Nicholson." It was pointless to prolong it any longer. He lifts his head and knocks on the door.

Brett walks in and sees Eric and Zach working on the little red guitar. The somber look on his face turns to one of anger as all his emotions collide. "What's going on here?!?"

Zach looks up in surprise. "Dad!"

Brett looks at the guitar. "What's my guitar doing here?!?"

"I was gonna tell you. I..."

Brett takes the guitar off the bed. "This wasn't yours to play with, Zach! It's not a toy!"

"I know, dad, I'm sorry. I was trying to fix it." Zach tries to hold back his tears.

Eric jumps in, "It just needs to dry."

Brett looks at Eric. "I'm talking to my son!"

"Don't yell at him! He's the one who fixed it!"

Brett takes in the image of his son sitting beside his father. The timing on this was all off. "Let's go."

"No!"

"*Now,* Zach!"

Zach stands, "I told you I didn't mean to do it!" Zach runs out of the room; Eric rises.

"You stay right where you are! This is between me and my son!"

Brett takes the guitar and heads out of the room. Eric, emotionally distraught, stands in the middle of the room unsure of what to do with himself.

Ray is standing in the hallway when he sees Brett running after Zach in the opposite direction. He turns and walks into Eric's room carrying the wooden bear in his hand.

*   *   *

Zach sits on a bed in an empty patient room, crying. Brett enters and sets the red guitar down; he sits down beside him. "Hey…"

Zach does not respond.

"I shouldn't have flown off the handle like that. I'm sorry, Zach."

Zach looks up.

"I haven't been doing a good job lately of paying attention to you—or keeping my promises. When I was your age, I always wanted my father to spend time with me. When I had you guys, I promised myself that I would be the kind of dad that made my kids feel important. I haven't been doing a very good job of that, have I?"

"I didn't mean to break your guitar."

"It's okay." Brett picks it up off the ground. "It look as good as new. I should've given this to you a long time ago." He hands the guitar over to Zach. "It's all yours."

Zach holds it delicately.

"What do you think about me teaching you to write some songs to play?"

A huge smile spreads onto Zach's face. "That's what I put on my Christmas list."

"What? Me teaching you to write songs?"

"No. You spending time with me."

Brett is overcome by his son's revelation. "I love you, Zach."

"Love you too..."

Brett holds him close.

Bess runs in, "There you are!" Brett and Zach look up. Bess is standing in the doorway. "You need to get dressed. Your sister is having a fit. We can't have a Christmas play without Joseph!" Zach smiles and heads out the door. He stops and turns. "You coming?"

"I'll be right there."

Bess and Zach head down the hall. Brett looks out the window reminded of one simple thing—nobody was perfect. He had hoped to meet his father one day, but these were not the circumstances under which he imagined it. But at least...it was a circumstance.

He gets up and walks back toward Eric's room. Eric is sitting on his bed holding the wooden bear in his hands. He looks at Brett as the tears stream down his face. Brett cannot comprehend how Eric came across the figurine. Both men look at one another in silence, knowing who each one was to each other, and that the other one knew it too. "It's you..."

Brett nods his head as tears fill his eyes.

But just as suddenly as the recognition comes, it slowly fades. Brett watches as Eric's face shifts from one of clarity to one of confusion. Eric looks down at the figurine in his hand, not understanding how it got there. He looks around the room, "Where is my guitar?"

Brett feels the ache in his heart the moment he sees the shift. He moves toward his father and grabs for the guitar. "Here it is."

Eric looks at him with vacant eyes. "Thank you." Eric continues to stare at him. "Do you think he'll forgive me? My son?"

Brett can no longer keep his emotions inside. Tears stream down his face as he answers, "He already has."

There is a slight knock on the door. Brett turns and sees Rebecca. The moment she sees the look on his face, she touches his cheek in understanding. She leans over and speaks to Eric, "Mr. Reynolds, how would you like to see a Christmas play?"

He looks off in the distance, "Okay."

He slowly rises. Rebecca loops her arm through his. She grabs hold of Brett's hand; they slowly head down the hall.

* * *

Rebecca, Brett and Eric enter the room just as the kids finish the last verse of *Silent Night*. Gabby plays the role of Mary, while Zach plays Joseph. They kneel side by side looking down at the manger where a doll representing Baby Jesus resides. Brett helps Eric sit down in a nearby chair. Brett looks down at him as Eric takes in the wonderment of the scene before him. Brett looks up and sees his children. Rebecca comes up beside him and touches his arm. She rests her head against his shoulder.

Ray stands in the back of the room taking it all in.

As the song ends, a young ten-year-old boy steps forward from the group of singers behind the Nativity scene and reads from a piece of paper, "And behold, an angel of the Lord stood before them..."

Effie stands near the steps at the bottom of the stage while the boy continues on; Beth is beside her dressed in an angel costume. Effie leans over her cane and whispers, "You're on."

Beth nods and quietly walks up the steps.

"Then the angel said to them, 'Do not be afraid'..."

Beth stops and shouts at the boy, "BE FEARLESS!"

Ray smiles with pride.

The young boy doesn't know what to do. He looks at Effie.

She whispers to him, "Keep going..."

He nods and continues on while Beth makes her way across the stage and over to Baby Jesus. "For unto you is born this day in the city of David a Savior who is Christ the Lord." He looks up at the crowd and smiles at his mom—Sarah Bielski. She smiles and waves back.

Beth kneels down in front of the manger and puts her two tiny hands together in prayer. The room is utterly silent. Rebecca leans back against Brett as he wraps his arms around her. Beth looks down at the Baby Jesus. She cocks her head to the side and starts singing, *"Happy Birthday to you, Happy Birthday to you..."*

While her innocent voice fills the room, the faces of the families and patients soften as the tiny angel before them sings on, *"Happy Birthday, dear Jesus, Happy Birthday to you..."*

Effie watches with tear-filled eyes, deeply touched and reminded of the little sister she once loved.

Sarah holds her mother Agnes' hand. Agnes squeezes it. Sarah looks up at her mother in surprise. Agnes turns her head and looks at Sarah—there is recognition in her eyes. She smiles at her daughter. "I love you, Sarah."

Sarah stares at her, "I love you too, mom. Merry Christmas."

"Merry Christmas." Agnes looks back at Beth singing on stage.

Beth leans in and whispers to Baby Jesus, "When I grow up, I hope I'll be like you someday..."

Ray is the only one who hears her faithful wish. He smiles fondly, remembering that first Christmas. There were no twinkling lights or Christmas trees then, no elves or snowmen. There was a stable filled with hay, swaddling clothes, and a manger. But had there been a little girl such as Beth singing to the one true king, the way she was singing now, he knew he would have fallen to his knees once again.

A single beam of light shines down brightly on Beth and the manger. Rebecca looks up at the stage lights. "Where is that light coming from?"

Ray's face is one of pride as he looks at Beth up on stage. Beth smiles at Baby Jesus and stands to face the crowd. All the children shout in unison, "Merry Christmas to all...and..." The words get mumbled as half the kids forget the lines. Gabby finishes it, "A good night!"

She looks at Zach. "How could you forget? It's the same line as last year!"

Zach shrugs. Bess runs on stage and waves her arms for everyone to stay seated. "Wait, wait, we have one more song before we let you all get back to your visiting." She looks into the crowd. She smiles widely the moment she finds who she's looking for. "BRETT!!!"

Brett freezes. Rebecca looks up at him.

"Brett! Come on up here!"

Brett shakes his head.

"Yes, you! Zach told me you have a song."

Brett looks at Zach in utter shock.

"Come on, dad!"

Rebecca nudges him. "You'd better get up there."

"But I don't have a song..."

She pushes him forward. "You have a ton. Now get!"

He stumbles backward. "But I don't have a guitar."

"Take mine."

Brett turns and sees Eric standing in front of him; he holds his guitar out to Brett. Brett stares at him. Eric still has the lost look on his face. "Thank you."

Brett makes his way up on stage. He looks out at the elderly patients; some sitting with their families, others all alone. He looks at his children on stage beside him. He steps forward. "Um, I, uh, wasn't planning on singing. But I made a promise to write a song this Christmas." He looks across the room to Rebecca. "This one's for my wife. Merry Christmas, Rebecca." He strums his guitar.

> *Here under the tree I think of all that could be*
> *And I'm thankful for my life*
> *I'm sorry I could not see what you mean to me*
> *My love, my heart my wife.*

Brett and Rebecca's eyes meet from across the room.

> *There are too many promises I never kept*
> *Too many things I would just say*
> *And all the pain I put you through*
> *I wish that I could take it all away.*

He looks at his children standing beside him, seeing the blessings that surround him.

> *There is a guiding star*
> *That leads you to a place*
> *Of love of peace and grace*
> *And when I see that star*
> *I know where you are because that's*
> *When I see your face*
> *In every way, I say today, thank you.*
> *It's a wonderful life.*
>
> *I don't need fame, no one to know my name,*
> *Just home and my family*
> *I could look in places, those millions of faces*
> *But your face is now all I see*
> *I was looking for meaning of why*

Eric looks up at Brett with wonderment.

> *A reason for all that I do*
> *And I found that reasons been here all the time*
> *And baby that reason is you.*

Sarah and Agnes hold each other as he plays and sings; Gertie taps her feet to the tune.

There is a guiding star
That leads you to a place
Of love of peace and grace
And when I see that star
I know where you are because that's
When I see your face
In every way, I say today,
Becca, thank you for being my wife
I love you. It's a wonderful life.

As Brett finishes his song, the crowd applauds. Beth dives into Brett's legs and gives him a hug. Bess rushes back on stage, "Merry Christmas, everybody!"

As Bess descends the stairs, a handsome, older gentleman extends his hand to help her down.

"Oh, why, thank you. It's so nice to know there are still gentlemen alive in this world."

"My pleasure. I was just here to visit a cousin of mine." He gives her his arm.

"Which cousin?"

"Don Jones."

"Oh, Don! Yes! He's one of my favorite patients."

He looks at her scrubs, "And violet is my favorite color. I was just telling this fellow, Ray, that I had to meet the woman wearing my favorite color. He sent me right on over."

"Ray is a good man." As they walk on, Bess looks up to heaven and mouths the words, "Thank you, Jesus."

Brett descends the stairs carrying Beth on his back. Eric walks up to Brett. "Mister, that was *great!* Almost like you knew just what my soul needed."

Brett nods, too overcome for words. Eric walks away with a lost look on his face as he looks at all the unfamiliar surroundings.

"That's just what my soul needed too."

Brett looks over and sees Rebecca. "Nicely done, Nicholson. I got my Christmas wish." She leans in and gives him a kiss.

Beth climbs off of Brett and jumps off the stage. Zach comes up beside his parents, "I'm gonna go give Mr. Reynolds his guitar back."

Brett looks up and sees Eric walking slowly down the hall. "I'll go with you."

Rebecca watches as Brett and Zach head over to Eric, a concerned look is on her face. Brett touches Eric's arm and gives him back his guitar. "Mr. Reynolds!" Zach notices the far-off look on Eric's face and is thrown off by his demeanor.

"Zach, why don't you tell your mom to get your things so we can head out?"

"Okay."

Brett extends his arm to Eric. "Why don't I help you back to your room."

Eric nods and gently grabs hold of Brett's arm. Zach wraps his arms around Rebecca, "What's wrong with Mr. Reynolds?"

Rebecca holds him close. "It's what happens sometimes with Alzheimer's patients...they forget where they are and who they are. Come on. Let's get your things so we can go home."

They head down the hall. Rebecca looks back at father and son one last time and walks on.

Beth runs over to the back of the room toward Ray. He crouches down to her as she approaches.

"I was fearless!"

"Yes, you were. You were a perfect angel." He hands her the wooden bear.

"Did you 'complish your mission?"

"Uh-huh." He looks at Brett and Eric as they walk out of the room. "The sad man was happy—even if it was for a moment."

Beth continues to stare at him. "Are you going back to heaven?"

Ray turns back to her and smiles faintly. "Yes, I am. Me and all the other angels like to celebrate Christmas too. We make a whole lot of noise singing songs to Jesus—just like you."

Beth giggles in reply. She leans in and wraps her tiny arms around Ray's neck and pulls him close. "I'm gonna miss you." She gives him a butterfly kiss. She releases her hold on Ray and runs down the hall after Zach and Rebecca. Ray watches her go, thinking only one thing, *An angel indeed.*

Effie watches all the families with the other patients. She shivers and rubs her arms, suddenly feeling cold. She turns and heads down the hall with the help of her cane. Effie continues walking down the hall when she passes a patient's room and sees a new orderly making up the bed. She stops and barks at the young man in the room. "Who are you?"

He turns and smiles. "I'm Joshua, the new orderly."

Effie is taken off-guard. "Where's Ray?"

"His last night was tonight. I just took over his shift. Getting the room ready for a new patient. I hear he's pretty feisty." Effie watches as he goes back to making up the room. "The other nursing home pretty much kicked him out."

She heads out of the room without saying a word, clearly upset with the news about Ray. The orderly looks up and sees she is gone. He goes back to making the bed.

Effie continues down the hall toward her room. As she passes the nameplate outside the new patient's door, it reads, "FREDDY MANNING." She does not see it as she moves on.

Bess calls after her, "Oh, Miss Effie!"

Effie turns.

"Now, I know you weren't going back to your room without your Christmas presents." Bess holds a basket of gifts and cards out for Effie. She's taken off-guard by the gesture.

"For me?"

"Yes, for you. You were a great help to me with the children's play. Now, come on. We'll take them to your room."

"Wait for me!"

They turn just as Gertie makes a beeline for them. She loops her arm through Effie's and Bess' as the three women head down the hallway side by side.

*   *   *

Later that night, Brett and Rebecca watched their children open their presents in frenzied excitement. Brett saw it all through different eyes as he watched his family gathered around the tree. He wanted be something great. He wanted to matter. He wanted to shine. And surrounded by his family—*he did*.

Gabby approaches him and hands him a gift, "It's from mom."

Rebecca rests her chin on Brett's shoulder as he unwraps his present. It was the music program. He looks at his beautiful wife knowing she must have worked an extra shift to afford this for him. He takes his finger and places it under her chin. He pulls her close and kisses her softly.

She gently touches his face. "Merry Christmas."

Chipper bursts into the room barking loudly; he is chasing a tiny dog. Gabby gasps, "A puppy! Yes!"

She and Zach dive for the dogs and are immediately met with licks. Beth opens one of her presents and pulls out an angel doll. She gasps and holds it close, swinging her body from side to side. "I love it!"

Zach rolls away from the puppy and crawls over to Rebecca. Without saying a word, she nods and hands Zach her phone. Zach scrolls through the phone and hands it to Brett. "Dad, this is my present to you."

Brett takes the phone. Zach instructs him, "Hit play."

Brett hits the play button. It is a video of Zach holding the red guitar. Zach looks at the camera, "Merry Christmas, dad." He plays and sings the song to *Little Red Guitar*. Brett watches his son sing the entire song. When it ends, he merely looks at his son with pride.

"I finished your last verse. Actually, Mr. Reynolds helped me."

Rebecca places her hands gently on her husband's shoulders. A moment passes between father and son. "Come here."

Zach walks over and sits down between Brett and Rebecca. "I'm sure it wasn't as good as you would've done."

Brett puts his arm around his son and looks him dead in the eye, "It was better than anyone could've done—even me. You were great."

Brett kisses the top of his son's head.

The clock suddenly strikes midnight.

Chipper is posed in front of Gabby. He turns his head from the clock to Gabby and barks, "I LOVE YOU!"

Everyone stops and stares at Chipper.

Beth shouts, "I knew it!"

Gabby is stunned, "Dogs *can* talk...dogs can talk!"

Beth hugs her angel doll tightly, "I told you, Ray never lies."

* * *

Ray stood in front of the Nativity scene, smiling down at the baby Jesus lying in the manger. He had been sent to Snow Falls to answer the prayer of one man, knowing that the answer of one would be the answer of many.

Mission accomplished.

He could feel it in the air—the hope, the joy, and most of all...the love. Christmas is a time of traditions, gatherings and preparation, but most of all it is a time where the spirit of the weary soul is heard—and it is heard by all. And there is no greater gift than the Father's love.

"Glory to God in the highest..."

Ray looks up at the heavens.

"And peace to his people on earth." He nods in salute to the angel statue and walks down the middle of Main Street. As he does, the darkened windows light up one...by...one.

ABOUT THE AUTHORS

Corina Marie Zurcher is the author of the children's books *Growing Up Claus* and *Hailey the Courageous*, as well as the fantasy novels *Archangels, The Father of Lights* and the upcoming novel *Legacy*. She is also an actress, screenwriter and producer. *Snow Falls* is the novelization of the screenplay. Visit her website www.nevermorepublications.com. You can also join her on Facebook and Tumblr.

Maryann Costa Beckman is a writer specializing in web copy, script writing, poetry and fiction. Her other works, *The Secret of the Box, The People of Advent* and *The Journey of the Magi*, are also inspirational works of fiction and poetry that the whole family will enjoy. Maryann has written reviews and copy for numerous publications and websites. A graduate of Franciscan University with a Master's Degree in Business Administration, she lives in Southern California with her husband Joshua and is always at work on her next novel.

Ray Fontenault is an independent songwriter and the owner of DoRay Music Promotions. He is a member of BMI, the Rhode Island Songwriters Association, and is one of the owners at Songramp.com. Ray enjoys relationships with several publishing firms and is an award winning songwriter for his song *Solid Rock*, taking 1st place in the "Cashing The Stars" songwriting contest. Ray continues to promote his songs and is always looking for quality artists to cut his songs. To find out more about Ray and hear his songs, visit: www.doraymusicpromotions.com.